Unearthly Fantasy...

He had an odd feeling, one of dissociation. It lasted for only two seconds, then it was gone, but during that time he knew that something alien, something unearthly, had occurred.

Two Hawks turned to O'Brien: "You ever read much science fiction?"

"Naw. That goofy stuff."

"Better for you if you had. You might have a more flexible mind. The point is, the science fiction fantasy of parallel universes has become for us a reality. Somehow, we've passed into another universe. We're on Earth, but not the one we knew."

TOMORROW'S WORLD

through the minds of

TODAY'S BEST WRITERS

EDMOND HAMILTON

LESTER DEL REY   JAMES BLISH

PHILIP K. DICK   POUL ANDERSON

RAYMOND C. JONES   ROBERT SILVERBERG

MACK REYNOLDS   MURRAY LEINSTER

M. C. PEASE FRANK BELKNAP LONG EANDO BINDER

and

BELMONT SCIENCE FICTION

THIS STRANGE TOMORROW

ANTON YORK, IMMORTAL

THE SCHEME OF THINGS

TIME OUT OF JOINT

OF GODLIKE POWER

SPACE PLATFORM

THE ALIEN

DOOMSTAR

THE
GATE
OF TIME

by
Philip Jose Farmer

Belmont Books • New York City

THE GATE OF TIME

A Belmont Book—May 1970

Published by
Belmont Productions, Inc.
185 Madison Avenue, New York, N.Y. 10016

PRINTED IN THE UNITED STATES OF AMERICA

THE
GATE
OF TIME

A year after the war, my publisher sent me to Stavanger, Norway, to interview Roger Two Hawks. I had full authority to negotiate a contract with him. The terms were very favorable, especially when the lack of printing facilities and distribution of that postwar period is considered. I had asked for the assignment, since I had heard so much about Roger Two Hawks. Most of the stories were incredible, even contradictory yet my informants swore to the truth of their testimonies.

So high-pitched was my curiosity, I would have quit my job and gone on my own to Norway if my publisher had refused me. And this was at a time when jobs in my field were not easy to get. Rebuilding our destroyed civilization was the foremost goal; craftsmanship in steelworking or bricklaying was more desired than facility with the pen.

Nevertheless, people were buying books, and there was a worldwide interest in the mysterious stranger, Roger Two Hawks. Everyone had heard of him, but those who had known him well were either dead or missing.

I booked passage on an old steamer that took five days to get to Stavanger. I did not even wait to check in at the hotel, since it was late evening. Instead, I asked directions, in my abominable Norwegian, to the hotel at which I knew Two Hawks was staying. I had tried to get reservations there with no success.

The taxi fare was very high, since fuel was still being rationed. We drove through many dark streets with unlit gaslights. But the front of the hotel was brightly illuminated, and the lobby was crowded with noisy and laughing guests, still happy about having lived through the war.

I asked the desk clerk for Two Hawks' room and was told that he was in the ballroom, attending a large party given by the mayor of Stavanger.

I had no trouble locating Roger Two Hawks, since I had seen many photographs of him. He stood at one corner of the

7

room, surrounded by men and women. I pushed my way through them and soon stood near him. He was a tall well-built man with a handsome, although aquiline, face. His hair was a dark brown; his skin was dark although not much darker than that of some of the Norwegians present. But his eyes were unexpectedly grey, as cool and grey as a winter Icelandic sky. He was holding a drink of Norland in one hand and chatting away with frequent flashings of his white teeth. His Norwegian was no better than mine, that is, fluent but heavily accented and not always grammatically acceptable. Beside him stood a beautiful blonde whom I also recognized from photographs. She was his wife.

When a short pause came in the conversation, I took the opportunity to introduce myself. He had heard of me and my visit, of course, because both my publisher and myself had corresponded with him. His voice was a deep rich baritone, very pleasant and at the same time confidence-inspiring.

He asked me how my trip was, and I told him that it was endurable. He smiled and said, "I had begun to think that your publisher had changed his mind and you weren't coming after all. Apparently, the wireless had also broken down on your ship."

"Everything did," I said. "The vessel was used for coastal shipping during the war and was bombed at least four times. Some of the repairs were pretty hasty and done with shoddy materials."

"I'm leaving Norway in two days," he said abruptly. "That means that I can give you about a day and a half. I'll have to tell you the story and depend on you to get it right. How's your memory?"

"Photographic," I replied. "Very well. But that means that neither of us will get much sleep. I'm tired, but I'd like to start as soon as possible. So. . . ?"

"Right now. I'll tell my wife we're going up to my room and I'll be a moment explaining to my host."

Five minutes later, we were in his room. He put on a big pot of coffee while I got the contract and my pen and notebook out. Then he said, "I really don't know why I'm doing this. Perhaps I'd like . . . well, never mind. The point is, I need money and this book seems to be the easiest way to get it. Yet, I may not come back to collect any royalties. It all depends on what happens at the end of my voyage."

I raised my eyebrows but said nothing. With one of the quick yet fluid motions characteristic of him, he left my side and strode across the room to a large table. On it was a globe of the world, a prewar model that did not show the change in boundaries that had taken place in the past year.

"Come here a moment," he said. "I want to show you where my story begins."

I rose and went to his side. He turned the globe slowly, then stopped it. With the point of a pencil, he indicated a spot on the land a little to the left of the central western shore of the Black Sea.

"Ploesti, Rumania," he said. "That's where I'll begin. I could start much farther back, but to do that would take time which we don't have. If you have any questions about my story before then, you'll have to insert them whenever you get the chance. However, I have a manuscript which outlines my life before I went on the mission against the oil-fields of Ploesti."

"Ploesti, Rumania?" I said.

"Ploesti, the great oil-producing and refining heart of Deutschland's new empire. The target of the 9th Air Force, based in Cyrenaica, North Africa. It took five years of war before the Americans could launch an attack against the life-blood of Germany's transportation and military effectiveness. Overloaded with bombs, ammunition, and gasoline, 175 four-motored bombers set out to destroy the oil tanks and refineries of Ploesti. We did not know that it was called *Festung* Ploesti, Fortress Ploesti, that the greatest concentration of anti-aircraft guns in Europe ringed that city. Nor would it have made much difference if we had known, except that we might not have been so shocked when we found out.

"I was first pilot on the *Hiawatha*; my co-pilot was Jim Andrews. He was from Birmingham, Alabama, but the fact that I was part Iroquois Indian didn't seem to bother him any. We were the best of friends."

He stopped, then smiled, and said, "By the way, you are looking at Ye Compleat Iroquoian. I have ancestors from every existing Iroquois tribe, including great-grandparents from the Iroquoian-speaking Cherokees. But my father was part Icelandic and my mother was part Scotch."

I shrugged and said, to explain my blank look, "Can I expect to get some explanation of this from the manuscript you spoke of?"

"Yeah, sure. Anyway . . ."

1

THE MISSION leader of the group had taken the wrong turn at Targoviste. Instead of heading for Ploesti, the Circus was going toward Bucharest. First Lieutenant Two Hawks realized the error and, like some of the other pilots, he disobeyed orders by breaking radio silence. There was no reply from the mission leader, who steadfastly kept on the wrong road. Then, far to their left, Two Hawks saw a smudge in the mist and knew that this had to be smoke from burning refineries. Other groups had gotten to the correct destination, and had released their bombs.

He looked at the lead bomber and wondered if the colonel had also seen the telltale smoke. Suddenly, the lead plane turned at right angles to the course and headed toward the smoke. Two Hawks, with the others, turned his plane in a maneuver so tightly executed that formation was maintained as strictly as before. The *Hiawatha,* engines straining to push at two hundred and forty-five mph, swept at only fifty feet above the ground. Sections of high green corn, alfalfa, and sheafs of wheat in gleaming stubble flashed below him. Ahead of the group, out of the smoke, the cables and elephantine bodies of barrage balloons hovered. Some were rising from the ground, and those at a high altitude were being pulled down to counter the low altitude attack.

Two Hawks felt dismay, although he did not say anything to Andrews. The planes were coming in from the wrong direction, so that all the weeks of intensive briefing on identification of targets was wasted. Approaching from this angle would make everything unrecognizable.

The road to Ploesti was twenty-five miles long and took five minutes to cover. Long before the end of the goal was reached, the Germans sprung the trap. Sides of haystacks exploded to reveal 20 mm. and 37 mm. guns. The freight cars on the railway sidings fell apart, and the 37 mm. cannons previously hidden began to flash. The fields themselves suddenly exposed pits containing madly firing machine guns. Ahead, 88 mm. and 105 mm. monsters, firing pointblank with short-fused shells, made the air a white-and-black gauntlet. The red business for which the attackers and defenders had prepared so long was now begun.

The *Hiawatha* shuddered at the burst of the great shells and then trembled as her own gunners opened fire on the AA batteries with their twin .50's. The air was woven with a drunken pattern of tracers and poignettes, so thickly intertwined it seemed that no aircraft could get through without being struck many times. The uproar was ear-shattering with the bellow of 134 14-cylinder motors, explosions from 88's fired only a few yards away, the shock of shrapnel blasts, and the insane chatter of the two hundred and thirty machine guns in the B-24's themselves.

Roger Two Hawks kept formation and the fifty-foot height from the ground, but he also managed sidelong flicks of his gaze. To one side, on a crossroad, the muzzle of an 88 flashed, and he could see the dark blurred bulk of the projectile flying towards its rendezvous. He pushed the wheel forward and dived a little, dropping to within twenty feet of the hurtling ground. The shell went harmlessly by.

Refinery tanks exploded ahead, Himalayas of flame arose, and he eased the *Hiawatha* back to fifty feet. It shook as a shell struck the tail but kept steadily on course instead of diving as he had expected. The tail gunner called in to report that the left aileron and left rudder were gone. The ship to Two Hawks' right looked as if a huge sword had slashed at it, but it was maintaining formation. The one on the left suddenly staggered, its nose enveloped in smoke, probably from a hit by an 88. It dropped like a hammer, slid burning into the ground, rose upwards in many pieces, and then was enveloped in a huge ball of fire.

Pieces of aluminum and plexiglass, bright in the sun, rode by him. The smoke ahead parted to reveal tanks and towers shrouded in flames; a bomber, on fire, headed towards an untouched tank; another plane began to turn over, its two port engines flaming; a third, also aflame, rose to gain altitude so that its crew could try to parachute. A fourth, to the right, released its bombs, and these plumeted down striking several tanks, all of which exploded into flame; one took the bomber with it. The huge ship, splitting in two, and also cartwheeling, soared out from the smoke and smashed into an untouched tank. This went up with a blast that seized the *Hiawatha* and hurled it upwards. Two Hawks and Andrews fought the grip of the wind and regained control.

There was a maze of tanks, pipes, and towers ahead. Two Hawks pulled hard on the wheel and sent the *Hiawatha* upwards to avoid striking the towers. He yelled at Andrews, "Dump the bombs!"

Andrews did not question his decision to make the release instead of waiting for the bombardier. He obeyed, and the plane rose up with increased power as the weight of the great bombs was gone. The end of a tower tore a hole down the center of the *Hiawatha*'s belly. But she flew on.

O'Brien, the topturret gunner, reported in his thick Irish brogue, "Gazzara's gone, sir! He and his turret just went down into the smoke."

"Tail-End Charlie's gone," said Two Hawks to Andrews.

"Hell, I didn't even feel the hit!" Andrews said. "You feel the shell?"

Two Hawks did not reply. He had already sent the *Hiawatha* down to avoid the murderous barrage above the fifty-foot level. He drove the ship between two tanks which were so close together that only a foot or so of space existed between each wingtip and a tank. But he was forced to bring her up again so fast she seemed to stand on her tail to get over a radio tower, the tip of which was wagging like a dog's tail from the flak bursts.

Andrews said, "God! I don't think we can make it!"

Two Hawks did not reply. He was too busy. He banked the plane to lift his right wing and so avoided collision with the top of the tower.

The ship shuddered again; an explosion deafened him. Wind howled through the cockpit. A hole had appeared in the plexiglass in front of Andrews, and he was slumped forward, his face a blur of torn flesh, sheared bone, and spurting blood.

Two Hawks turned the *Hiawatha* east but, before the maneuver was completed, the ship was struck again in several places. Somebody in the aft was screaming so loudly that he could be heard even above the cacophony outside and the air shrilling through the holes in the skin of the craft. Two Hawks pulled the *Hiawatha* up at as steep an angle as he dared. Even though he had to go through the fiery lacework ahead, he had to get altitude. With his two port engines on fire and the propeller of the outermost starboard engine blown off, he could not stay airborne much longer. Get as high as possible and then jump.

He had an odd feeling, one of dissocation. It lasted for only two seconds, then it was gone, but during that time he knew that something alien, something unearthly, had occurred. What was peculiar was the sensation that the dissociation was not just subjective; he was convinced that the ship itself and all it contained had been wrenched out of the context of normality—or of reality.

Then he forgot the feeling. The spiderweb of tracers and stars of flak parted for a moment, and he was above it and through it. The roar and crump of the exploding shells were gone; only the wind whistling through the hole in the shield could be heard.

From nowhere, a fighter plane appeared. It came so swiftly, as if out of a trapdoor in the sky, that he had no time to identify it. It flashed by like black lightning, its cannon and machine guns spitting. The two craft were so close that they could not avoid each other; the German flipped one wing and dived to get away. The ship staggered again, this time struck its death blow. The left wing was sheared off; it floated away with he right wing of the German fighter.

A moment later, Two Hawks was free of the *Hiawatha*. The ground was so close that he did not wait the specified time to pull the ripcord but did so as soon as he thought he was free of the plane. He fell without turning over, and he saw that the city of Ploesti, as he knew it, was no longer there. Instead of the suburbs that had been below him, there were dirt roads, trees, and farms. Ploesti itself was so far away that it was nothing but a pillar of smoke.

Below him, the *Hiawatha*, now a globe of flame, was falling. The German craft was turning over and over; a hundred yards away from it and a hundred feet above it, the parachute of the flier was unfolding, billowing out. Then his own chute had opened, and the shock of its grip on the air had seized him.

To his left, another man was swinging below his semi-balloon of silk. Two Hawks recognized the features of Pat O' Brien, the topturret gunner. Only two had escaped from the *Hiawatha*.

2

THE SNAP of the parachute, opening like a sail to catch the wind, made the straps cut into Two Hawks' legs. Something popped in his neck, but there was no pain. If anything, he thought briefly, the jerk and the popping of vertebrae had probably been more like an osteopathic treatment and had released tension in his body and straightened out his skeleton.

Then he was examining the terrain swelling below him, the details getting larger but the field of view getting smaller. His chute had opened only two hundred feet above the ground, so he did not have much time for study and very little time to get set for the drop.

The wind was carrying him at an estimated six miles an hour over a solid growth of trees. By the time he came to earth, he would be past it and in a field of cut wheat. Beyond the wheat field was a narrow dirt road running at right angles to him. Trees grew along the road, beyond which was a thatch-roofed cottage, a barnyard, and several small barns. Past the house was a garden surrounded by a log fence. Back of the garden, the trees grew in a single dense file a quarter of a mile wide. An opening in the trees permitted him to glimpse the darkness of a shadowy creek.

He came down closer to the trees than he had thought he would because there was an unexpected lull in the wind. His feet brushed the top of a tree on the edge of the woods, then he was on the ground and rolling. Immediately, he was up on his feet and going through the required procedure for disentangling himself. The trees stopped whatever wind there might be; the chute had collapsed on the ground.

He unsnapped the straps and began to roll his chute into a ball. O'Brien was doing the same thing. Having collected the silk, Two Hawks picked it up and jogged towards O'Brien, who was running towards him. O'Brien said excitedly, "Did you see those soldiers over to the left?"

Two Hawks shook his head. "No. Were they coming our way?"

"They were on a road at right angles to this one. Must be a main road, although it wasn't paved. They were too far away for me to get many details. But they sure looked funny."

"Funny?"

O'Brien removed his helmet. He ran a thick stubby hand, freckled and covered with pale red hairs, through his orange mop. "Yeah. They had a lot of wagons drawn by oxen. There were a couple of cars at the head, but they didn't look like any cars I ever seen. One was an armored car; reminded me of the pictures of cars like in that old book my Dad had about World War I."

O'Brien grinned toothily. "You know. The Great War. The Big War. The Real War."

Two Hawks did not comment. He had heard O'Brien talk about his father's attitude towards the present conflict.

"Let's get into the woods and bury this stuff," he said. "You get a chance to bring any survival stuff with you?"

Two Hawks led the way into the thick underbrush. O'Brien shook his head, "I was lucky to get out with my skin. Did any of the others make it?"

"I don't think so," Two Hawks said. "I didn't see any-body."

He pushed on into the woods. His legs and arms were shaking, and something inside him was trembling also. Reaction, he told himself. It was natural, and he would be all right as soon as he got a chance to get hold of himself. Only thing was, he might not get a chance. The Germans or the Rumanians would be sending out search parties now. Probably, the peasants living in the house on the other side of the road had seen them drop, although it was possible that no one had. But if they had watched the big American ship burning and falling, and had seen the two chutists, they might be phoning in now to the nearest garrison or the police post.

He had been on his hands and knees, covering his chute with dirt in a depression between two huge tree-roots. Abruptly, he straightened up, grunting as if hit in the pit of his stomach. It just occurred to him that he had not seen a single telephone wire during his drop. Nor had he seen any electrical transmission towers or wires. This was strange. The absence of these would not have been peculiar if the plane had gone down out in the sticks. Rumania was not a very well developed country. But the *Hiawatha* must not have been more than five miles from the refineries in Ploesti when it had encountered the German fighter.

Moreover, where were the suburbs that had been below him only a minute before he had experienced that twisting feeling? One moment they were there; the next, gone. And there was something peculiar also about the suddenness with which the German had appeared. He could swear that it had dropped out of the sky itself.

They finished covering up the chutes. Two Hawks stripped off his heavy suit and at once felt cooler. There was a slight breeze, which meant that the wind must have sprung up again outside the woods. O'Brien already had his suit off. He wiped his freckled forehead and said, "It sure is quiet, ain't it? Hell of a lot quieter than it's going to be, huh?"

"You got a gun?" Two Hawks asked.

O'Brien shook his head and pointed at the .32 automatic in the holster at Two Hawks' side. "That isn't much of a gun," he said. "How many bullets you got?"

"Five loaded. Twenty more in my pocket," Two Hawks said. He did not mention the two-barreled derringer in the little holster on the inside of his belt in back nor the switchblade knife in his pocket.

"Well, it's better than nothing," O'Brien said.

"Not much better." Two Hawks was silent for a moment, conscious that O'Brien was watching him with expectation. It was evident he was not going to offer any suggestions. That was as it should be, since Two Hawks was the officer. But Two Hawks doubted that O'Brien would have anything helpful to say even if he were asked to do so.

It struck Two Hawks then that he knew very little about O'Brien except that he was a steady man during a mission, had been born in Dublin, and had emigrated to America when he was eleven years old. Since then, he had lived in Chicago.

Finally, O'Brien said, "I'm sure glad you're with me. You're an Indian and you been raised in the country. I don't know what the hell to do in all these trees. I'm lost."

By then, Two Hawks had the map out of the pocket of his jacket. He did not think it would help O'Brien's morale to tell him that his officer, the Indian, had been raised in the country and knew the woods there, but he did not know this country or these woods.

Two Hawks spread the map out and discussed the best

routes of escape. After a half hour, during which they took off their jackets and unbuttoned their shirts because of the heat, they had picked several avenues of flight. Whichever one they took, they would travel at night and hole up during the day.

"Let's go back to the edge of the woods so we can watch the road," Two Hawks said. "And the farmhouse. If we're lucky, we weren't seen. But if some peasant has told the local constabulary, they'll be searching these woods for us soon. Maybe we better get out of here. Just in case. In fact, we will if the coast looks clear."

They sat behind a thick bush, in the shadows cast by a huge pine, and watched the road and the farmhouse. A half-hour passed while they swatted at mosquitoes and midges, handicapped by having to strike softly so they would not make slapping noises. They saw no human beings. The only sound was that of the wind shushing through the treetops, the distant barking of a dog, and the bellowing of a bull from beyond the farmhouse.

Two Hawks sat patiently, only moving to speed the circulation in his legs, cramped from sitting still. O'Brien fidgeted, coughed softly, and started to take a pack of cigarettes out of his shirt pocket. Two Hawks said, "No smoking. Somebody might see the smoke. Or even smell the tobacco."

"From this distance?" O'Brien said.

"Not likely, but we don't want to take any chances," Two Hawks replied. For another half-hour, he continued to watch. O'Brien groaned softly, whistled between his teeth, shifted back and forth, then began to rock on the base of his spine. "You'd make a hell of a poor hunter," Two Hawks said.

"I ain't an Indian," O'Brien said. "I'm just a city boy."

"We're not in the city. So try practising some patience."

He sat for fifteen minutes more, then said, "Let's get over to the house. Looks deserted. Maybe we could get some food and be on our way into the woods on the other side of the house."

"Whose getting ants in their pants now?" O'Brien said.

Two Hawks did not reply. He rose and took the switchblade from his pocket and stuck it between the front of his belt and his belly. He walked on ahead of O'Brien, who seemed reluctant to leave the imagined safety of the woods. Before Two Hawks had gone ten yards, O'Brien had run up to him.

"Take it easy," Two Hawks said. "Act as if you had every

right to be here. Anybody seeing us from a long ways off might not think anything about it if we're casual."

There was a ditch between the edge of the field and the road. They leaped across the little stream in its bottom and walked across the dirt road. The ground was wet but not muddy, as if it had rained a few days ago. There were deep ruts, however, that looked like wagon tracks. And there were tracks of cattle and piles of excrement.

"No horses," Two Hawks said to himself. O'Brien said, "What?" But Two Hawks had opened the wooden gate and was ahead of him. He noticed that the hinges were also of wood, secured to the gate by wooden pins. The grass in the yard was short, kept so by several sheep with very fat tails. These raised their heads and then shied away but uttered no baas. Two Hawks wondered if they had vocal cords; it seemed unlikely that normal sheep would have been silent during the long time he had listened in the woods.

Now he could hear the clucking of hens from behind the house and the snort of some large animal in the barn. The house itself was built in the shape of an L with the long part of the leader facing the road. There was no porch. Big thick logs, the interstices between them chinked up by a whitish substance, formed the structure of the house. The roof was thatched.

On the smooth wood of the door was painted a crude representation of an eagle. Above it was painted a large open blue eye over which was a black X.

Two Hawks raised the wooden latch that locked the door and pushed in. He had no chance to follow his plan to walk boldly in. At that moment, a woman walked around the corner of the house. She gasped and stood still, staring at them with large brown eyes. Her brown skin turned pale.

Two Hawks smiled at her and greeted her in what he hoped was passable Rumanian. He had tried to gain some fluency in the language from a fellow officer of Rumanian descent while stationed in Tobruk, but he had not had time to master more than a few stock phrases and the names of some common items.

The woman looked puzzled, said something in an unfamiliar tongue, and then walked towards them. She had a rather pretty face, although her shape was a little too squat and her legs too thick for Two Hawks' taste. Her hair was blue-black, parted in the middle and plastered down with some sort of oil. Two braided pigtails hung down her back. She wore a necklace of red and tightly coiled seashells, an open-necked blouse of blue cotton, a wide belt of leather with a copper clasp, and a skirt of bright red cotton. It reached to her ankles. Her feet were bare and smeared with dirt, mud, and what looked like chicken excrement. A real peasant, thought Two Hawks. But if she's friendly, that's all that counts.

He tried some more Rumanian, got nowhere, and switched to German. She replied in the same guttural language she had used before. Although it did not sound Slavic to him, he spoke in Bulgarian. His knowledge of this was even more limited than his Rumanian. She evidently did not understand this either. However, she spoke the third time in a different speech than her first. This resembled Slavic; he tried again with Bulgarian, then with Russian, and Hungarian. She only shrugged and repeated the phrase. After hearing several more repetitions, Two Hawks understood that she was doing as he was, that is, trying out a foreign language of which she knew very little.

But when she saw that Two Hawks did not understand a word of it, she seemed to be relieved. She even smiled at him and then fell back into the first tongue she had used.

Two Hawks frowned. There was something familiar about it. Almost, he could catch a word here and there. Almost, but not quite.

He said to O'Brien, "We'll have to try sign language. I . . ."

He stopped; obviously alarmed, she was pointing past him. He turned just in time to catch the flash of sun from the metal of a vehicle through the trees. The forest was thin by the road, and he could see across another field, perhaps three hundred yards long, to a row of trees at right angles to him. This must line the road, which either turned there or was crossed by another road.

"Somebody coming in a car," he said. "We'd better take off. We'll have to trust this girl or else take her with us. And if we do that, we may have to kill her. In which case, we might as well do it now."

"No!" O'Brien said. "What the hell. . . !"

"Don't worry," Two Hawks said. "If we're captured, we might just end up in a prison camp. But if we kill the girl, we might get executed as common criminals."

The woman placed a hand on his wrist and pulled him to-

wards the corner of the house while she gestured with the
other hand and talked swiftly. It was evident that she wanted
to take them away from the approaching vehicle or perhaps
hide them.

Two Hawks shrugged and decided that there was little else
to do. If they took to the woods, they would soon be captured.
There just was not enough forest in which to hide.

They followed the woman around the corner and to the
back of the house. She led them inside, to the kitchen. There
was a huge stone fireplace with a log fire and a large iron pot
on a tripod above the fire. A savory odor rose from the simmering contents. Two Hawks had little time to examine the
kitchen; the woman lifted a trapdoor from the middle of the
bare wooden floor and gestured to them to go on down. Two
Hawks did not like the idea of placing himself and O'Brien in
a position from which he could not escape. But he either
could do that or take to the woods, and he had already rejected
that if something else was offered. He went down a flight of
ten steps with the Irishman close behind him. The trapdoor
was shut, and they were in complete darkness.

3

ABOVE THEM came the sound of something scraping across the floor. The woman was hiding the trapdoor with furniture. Two Hawks took out his flashlight and examined the room. His nose had already told him that there were strips of garlic and sausage and other food hanging from the roughly hewn beams above. There was a door close by; he pushed this open and then turned off the light. Enough light came through several chinks in the log wall of the house above for him to see. The large chamber was lined with shelves on which sat dust-covered glass jars. These contained preserved fruits, vegetables, and jellies. On the floor beneath the shelves were piles of junk; stuff the owner had not been able to throw away or else considered worth repairing some day. One item that particularly caught his attention was a large wooden mask, broken off at one corner. To examine it closer, he turned on his flashlight. It portrayed the face of a demon or a monster, painted in garish scarlet, purple, and a dead-white.

"I don't like being down here, Lieutenant," O'Brien said. He came close to Two Hawks as if he found comfort in the proximity. Although it was cool in the dark cellar, the Irishman was sweating. He stank of fear.

Then he said, "There's something funny as hell about all this. I meant to ask you, but I thought maybe you'd think I'd cracked. Did you feel as if you were being, well, sort of twisted. I got a sickish feeling, just before that German showed up. I thought I'd been hit at first. Then things got too exciting to think about it. But when we was back in the woods, sitting there, I got the same feeling. Only not so strong. Just feeling that there was something a lot more wrong than being shot down and hiding away from the krauts."

"Yeah, I had the same feeling, too," Two Hawks said. "But I can't explain it."

"I felt like, well, like Old Mother Earth herself had disappeared for a minute," O'Brien said. "How about that, huh?"

Two Hawks did not answer. He heard the vehicle approaching down the road, then stop in front of the house. The motor sounded like an old Model T. He directed the sergeant to help him pile junk beneath one of the chinks and then stood up on the unstable platform. The hole was only a little larger than his eye, but it permitted him to see the car and the soldiers getting out of it. It was a peculiar looking vehicle, perhaps not so much peculiar as old-fashioned. He remembered O'Brien's comment when they had first landed about the cars at the head of the ox-drawn wagon train.

Well, Rumania was supposed to be a very backward country, even if it had the largest and most modern oil refineries in Europe. And the soldiers certainly were not members of the Wehrmacht. On the other hand, their uniforms did not resemble anything in the illustrations he had seen during his briefings in Tobruk. The officer wore a shiny steel helmet shaped to look like a wolf's-head. There were even two steel ears. His knee-length jacket was a green-gray, but the collar had a strip of greyish animal fur sewed to it. There was an enormous gold-braided epaulette on each shoulder and a triple row of large shiny yellow buttons down the front of his jacket. His trousers were skintight, crimson, and had the head of a black bull on each leg just above the knees. He wore a broad leather belt with a holster. A strange-looking pistol was in his hand; he gestured with it while giving orders to his men in a Slavic-sounding speech. He turned and revealed that he was also wearing a sword in a scabbard on his left side. Shiny black calf-length boots completed his uniform.

Several of the soldiers were within Two Hawks' range of vision. They wore helmets that had a neck-protecting nape, but the shape above the head was cylindrical, like a steel plug hat. Their black coats came to the waist in front, then curved to make a split-tail in back that fell just below the back of the knees. They had baggy orange trousers and jackboots. There were swords in the scabbards hanging from broad belts and rifles in their hands. The rifles had revolving chambers for the cartridges, like some of the old Western rifles.

All had full beards and long hair except for the officer. He was a clean-shaven youth, blond and pale, certainly not a dark Rumanian type.

The men scattered. There were shouts from above, the tread of boots on the floors, and smashing sounds. The officer walked out of sight, but Two Hawks could hear him talking slowly, as if in a language he had been taught in school. The woman answered in the same speech, which had to be her native tongue. Two Hawks found himself straining to catch its meaning, almost but not quite succeeding. Ten minutes passed. The soldiers reassembled. Frightened squawks announced the "expropriation" of hens. A certain amount of stealing was to be expected, Two Hawks thought, but by the woman's own people? No, the soldiers could not be of the same nationality as she, otherwise there would be no language difficulty. Perhaps the woman belonged to one of the minorities of Rumania. It seemed logical, but he did not believe it.

Two Hawks waited. He could hear the soldiers laughing and talking loudly to each other. The woman was silent. About twenty minutes later, the officer apparently made up his mind that his men had had enough fun. He strode out of sight, and his voice came loudly to Two Hawks. Within a minute, the soldiers were lined up before him while he gave them a short but sharp lecture. Then they got into the car and drove off down the road.

"I don't think they were looking for us," Two Hawks said. They must know that the house has a cellar. But if not us, what were they looking for?"

He wanted to go out immediately, but he decided that the soldiers could be coming back up the road soon or another group could pass by. Better for the woman to tell them when it was safe. The day passed slowly. There was no sound from outside for a long while except for the clucking hens and mooing cows.

It was not until dusk that they heard furniture moving above the trapdoor. The door creaked open, and light from a lamp streamed through the oblong.

Two Hawks took the automatic from O'Brien and went up first, determined to shoot anybody waiting for them. Despite all the evidences of her trustworthiness, he still was not sure that she had not changed her mind and summoned the troops. It did not seem very likely since the soldiers would not have bothered waiting around until dusk. But you never knew, and it was better to take no chances.

There was a man standing in one corner of the kitchen and munching on a piece of dried meat. Two Hawks, seeing he was unarmed except for a big knife in a scabbard sheath, put his automatic in his belt. The man looked at them stonefacedly. He was as dark as the woman and had an eagle-like nose and high cheekbones. His straight black hair was cut in the shape of a helmet—a German helmet. His black shirt and dirty brown pants looked as if they were made of some coarse and tough cotton. His boots were dirty. He stank as if he had been sweating out in the fields all day. He looked old enough to be the woman's father and probably was.

The woman offered the two bowls of stew from the kettle still simmering in the fireplace. Neither was hungry, since they had been sampling the contents of the cellar. But Two Hawks thought it would be politic to accept. It was possible these people might believe that it was a gesture of hospitality and trust to offer a stranger food. They might believe that a man who ate under their roof was automatically sacrosanct. And the reverse could be true also. A stranger who accepted their bread would not break a tabu by harming them.

He explained this to O'Brien. While he was talking, he saw the farmer's expression break loose from its stony cast. He looked puzzled and frowned as if he thought there was something familiar about the language. However, he had no more success in translating than Two Hawks had had with their language.

The two aviators sat down at a five-legged table of smoothly planed but unvarnished pine. The woman served them, then busied herself working around the kitchen. She pumped water out of a handpump over the sink. Two Hawks felt a touch of nostalgia and homesickness at this, since it reminded him of the kitchen pump in his parents' farmhouse in upper New York when he had been a little boy. The man paced back and forth, talking to the woman, then sat down with the two and began eating from a large bowl. This was of ceramic with some symbols painted in blue on it. One of them was the likeness of the broken mask Two Hawks had seen in the cellar.

When he had finished eating, the farmer stood up abruptly and gestured at them to follow him. They stepped out through a swinging screen door with a mosquito net made of closely woven cotton fibers. Its interstices seemed too large to do its job, but the threads had been soaked in oil. Suddenly, Two Hawks recognized the odor. It was the same oil with which the woman had plastered her hair.

Although the oil was not sunflower seed oil, it triggered off a sequence of thought. Some of the older women on the

reservation near his father's farm had used sunseed oil on
their hair. His mind leaped at a conclusion which he could
only reject because it was incredible. But there was also the
undeniable fact that he now recognized the speech of the two
peasants as a form of very peculiar Iroquoian. It was still
largely unintelligible. But it was not Rumanian nor Hungarian
nor Slavic, neither Indo-European nor Ugro-Altaic. It was a
dialect related to the tongue of the Onondaga, the Seneca,
Mohawk, and the Cherokee. Not only in its phonology but
in its structure.

He said nothing to O'Brien but silently followed the man
and girl across the now dark barnyard. They passed an out-
house, and O'Brien made a request which Two Hawks tried to
pass on to the farmer. The man was impatient, but he agreed.
A few minutes later, they resumed their path to the barn.

O'Brien said, "We're really in the sticks. They don't have
no paper; there's a pile of clean rags and a bin for dirty ones.
They must wash them afterward. Geeze, and to think we was
eating from food she made. I bet she doesn't even wash her
hands!"

Two Hawks shrugged. He had more important matters to
think about then sanitation. The man opened the barndoors,
and they stepped inside.

The two large barndoors swung shut with a creaking of
wooden hinges. In the darkness, Two Hawks put his hand on
O'Brien's shoulder and pushed gently to urge him several feet
to the left. If the farmer planned to surprise them with an
attack, he would not find his victims where he had last seen
them. For about thirty seconds, there was no noise. Two Hawks
crouched down on the ground, O'Brien by his side. He closed
his fingers around the butt of his .32 and waited.

Then the farmer moved through the straw on the ground
away from Two Hawks. Slight metallic sounds made Two
Hawks wonder if blades, or maybe guns, were being taken
from a hiding place. Suddenly, a match flared, and he saw the
farmer applying the flame to the wick of a lantern. The wick
caught fire; the farmer adjusted the flow of oil; the interior
of the barn was cut into light and shadows.

The farmer, seeing them crouching on the ground, smiled
briefly. His smile seemed to indicate more of approval than
anything else. He gestured for them to follow him. They rose
and came after the farmer and the girl. Near the back of the
barn, a pig grunted from a stall. Large brown eyes looked at

them in the lantern light from behind wooden bars. Cows and pigs and sheep, thought Two Hawks, but no horses. Could the Germans have taken them all? Perhaps they had requisitioned all the horses of this particular farmer. But the photographs taken by reconnaissance planes before the raid had shown plenty of horses on Rumanian farms. And then there was O'Brien's brief sight of the column on the road. Cars and oxen-drawn wagons.

The farmer stopped before a shed built onto the back wall of the barn. He knocked three times, waited several seconds, knocked three times again, waited, and rapped three more times. The door swung open; the shack was dark inside. The two natives went inside, and the farmer gestured at them to come on in. As soon as the two fliers had entered, the door was closed, and the farmer turned up the lantern flame.

There were six people crowded inside the shed. The odor of dried sweat and rancid hair oil was strong. Four men, dark, eagle-faced, dressed in heavy cloth garments, were squatting or else leaning against the wall. All wore small round caps with single red feathers projecting from the top of each cap. Two had muzzle-loading, long-barreled muskets. One had a quiverful of arrows strapped to his back and a short recurved bow of horn in his fist. Two had the same type of rifles with revolving cartridge chambers that the soldiers had carried. All had long knives in scabbards at their belts; the handle of a tomahawk was thrust into the belt of one.

"Jeeze!" O'Brien said under his breath. He may have exclaimed because he was in a trap or because of the oddity and disparity of the weapons. More probably, he was startled by the sixth person, a woman. She was dressed in the same clothes as the others, but she was obviously not one of them. Her skin was very white, where there was no dirt, and her long hair was golden. She had a pretty although tired looking face with a snub nose and a sprinkling of faint freckles. Her eyes were large and deep blue.

Two Hawks, standing close to her, knew she had been in her clothes a long time. She stank, and her hands were dirty, the fingernails half-moons of filth. The whole group had the air and looks of fugitives. Or of guerrillas who had been a long time from their base.

The leader was a tall man with hollow cheeks and burning black eyes. His coarse black hair was cut to resemble the shape of a German helmet, and he wore heavy leather boots.

His shirt was of buckskin and hung outside his belt. The backs of his fists were tattooed with the faces of monsters or demons.

He spoke at length with the farmer and his daughter. Now and then he glanced sharply at the two Americans. Two Hawks listened with his ears tuned up. Occasionally, he could make a little sense out of the rapid firecracker explosions. Yes, the phonology was familiar, and so was a word or a phrase here and there. But he would never have understood anything if he had not had a fluent knowledge of all the Iroquoian languages, including Cherokee.

Once, the leader (his name was Dzikohses) turned to speak to the blonde. He used an entirely different language then, but it was one that also seemed vaguely familiar to Two Hawks. He was sure that it belonged to the Germanic family and that it was Scandinavian. Or was it? Now he could swear it was Low German.

Abruptly, Dzikohses focused his attention on O'Brien and Two Hawks. His index finger stabbing at them, occasionally indicating items of their uniforms, he rattled off one question after another. Two Hawks understood the pitches of interrogation, but he did not understand the questions themselves. He tried to reply in Onondaga, then Seneca, then Cherokee. Dzikohses listened with his eyebrows raised an a puzzled, sometimes irritated, expression. He switched to the same speech he had used with the blonde. Finding that this was not understood, he tried another language and worked his way through three others before Two Hawks could comprehend a word. The final attempt was in some form of Greek. Unfortunately, although Two Hawks had a fair reading knowledge of Homeric and Attic Greek, he had no conversational ability. Not that this knowledge would have helped him much, since Dzikohses' Greek seemed to be only distantly related to those that Two Hawks knew.

"What the hell's he gibbering about?" O'Brien growled.

"Ask him something in Gaelic," Two Hawks said.

"You nuts?" O'Brien replied, but he rattled off several sentences.

Dzikohses frowned and then threw his hands up as if to indicate that he was thrown for a complete loss. One thing Two Hawks was sure of, however. Dzikohses was no peasant. A linguist of his ability had to have traveled much or been well educated. And he bore himself as a man used to command.

Dzikohses became impatient. He gave several orders. The men checked their weapons; the girl pulled a revolver from under her loose foxskin jacket and examined the chambers. Dzikohses held out his hand for Two Hawks' automatic. Smiling, Two Hawks shook his head. Slowly, so that he would not startle the others or cause them to misinterpret his actions, he took his automatic from his holster. He ejected the clip of bullets and then reinserted them, making sure the safety was on before he put the gun back into the holster.

The eyes of the others widened, and there was a starburst of questions from them. Dzikohses told them to shut up. The farmer extinguished the lamp, and the whole group left the shed. Within two minutes, they were in the woods. The farmer and the daughter bade them a soft goodbye, then returned under the light of the half-moon to their house.

4

ALL NIGHT, the party followed a path that left the shadows of the trees only when necessary to cross fields to get from one woods to another. They saw nothing to disturb them and, shortly before dawn, they bedded down for the day in a broad hollow deep inside the forest. Their travel had been generally northeastward.

Before falling asleep under a pile of leaves, O'Brien asked Two Hawks if they were going towards Russia. Two Hawks said he thought so.

These people ain't Russians or Rumanians either," O'Brien said. "When I was a kid in Chicago, I lived in a neighborhood that had some Russkies and Rumanians, so I know these people ain't talking neither. What in hell are these gooks?"

"They're speaking some obscure dialect," Two Hawks said. He did not think that now was the time to spring some of his speculations on O'Brien. They would only confuse him. Besides, they were so fantastic, that he could not seriously entertain them himself.

O'Brien said, "You know something else that's funny? Back there at that farmer's, and on all the other farms we seen, there wasn't a single horse. You suppose the Krauts took them all?"

"Somebody did," Two Hawks said. "Better get to sleep. It's going to be a long tough night tomorrow."

It was also a long tough day. The huge mosquitoes that had made their life hell during the night did not go away with the daylight. When he could stand it no longer, Two Hawks awoke Dzikohses. With sign language, he made it apparent that he would now accept the offer he had previously turned down. He took the little bottle Dzikohses handed him and poured out a thin liquid. It had the vilest, most stomach-turning odor he had ever been unfortunate enough to whiff. But it kept the mosquitoes away. He smeared it over his face

and the back of his hands, then burrowed under the leaves.
The leaves protected the rest of him, since the needle-suckers
of the mosquitoes seemed to go through even his clothing. He
could understand now why the others wore such heavy garments even in the heat of summer. It was either suffer from
the heat, which was endurable, or go mad from the unendurable stabs of the mosquitoes.

Even shielded from the insects, he did not sleep heavily.
By noon, the woods became hot, and what with the sweat
encasing him and the sounds of men turning over, rustling the
leaves, or eliminating nearby, he woke frequently. Once, he
opened his eyes to see the hatchet face and black eyes of
Dzikohses over him. Two Hawks grinned at him and turned
over on his side. He was helpless; he could be disarmed or
killed at any time. But, so far, Dzikohses had shown no in-
clination to treat him as a possible enemy. Plainly, he was
puzzled by everything about the two strangers. No more puzzled by us than I am about him, Two Hawks thought, and slid
back into his bumpy sleep.

At dusk, they ate dried beef and hard black bread and
drank from canteens filled from a nearby creek. The men then
all faced east and took from their leather provision-packs
strings of beads and various carved wooden images. They
put the strings of beads around their necks and began telling
them with the left hands while they held the wooden images
up above their heads in their right hands. Their voices mur-
mured what seemed to be chants, although the chants were
not all the same. Two Hawks was startled by the image held
by the man nearest him. It was the head of a mammoth, its
proboscis curled aloft as if trumpeting, its long tusks curving
upward, its eyes little gems that glared red.

The men were standing up and facing east. The blonde
squatted, facing westwards. She, too, told beads, but did it
with her right hand. She had taken a silver stickpin from her
bag and driven it into the earth before her. Now, regarding
the image fixedly, her lips moved, and only by getting very
close to her could Two Hawks distinguish the words of her
slow measured speech. Now he heard a language none had
spoken before. It sounded Semitic to him, and he could have
sworn that he heard more than once words similar to the
Hebrew "Ba'al" and "Adoni." The silver image was a symbolic representation of a tree from which a man hung, the rope
around his neck tied with nine knots.

It was all very strange. O'Brien shivered and swore, crossed himself, and said a rapid Paternoster in a very low voice. Then he said, "Lieutenant, what kind of heathens have we fallen among?"

"I wish I knew," Two Hawks replied. "Anyway, let's not worry about their religion. If they get us to neutral territory, or to Russia, they've done their jobs."

The ceremonies took about three minutes. The beads and idols (if they were idols) were put away, the march was resumed. Not until midnight did they stop. Two men slipped into a village only a hundred yards away. They returned in fifteen minutes with more dried strips of beef, black bread, and six bottles of a very sour wine. All took a swig from the bottles, and then the fast walking was resumed. At dawn, as they bedded down, they heard the faroff boom of big cannon. Sometime late in the afternoon, Two Hawks was awakened by O'Brien. The Irishman pointed upwards through a break in the trees, and Two Hawks saw a huge silvery sausage shape passing at about a thousand feet overhead.

"That sure as hell looks like one of them dirigibles I read about when I was a kid," O'Brien said. "I didn't know the Krauts still had 'em."

"They don't," Two Hawks said.

"Yeah? How do you account for that, then? The Russians use 'em?"

"Maybe," Two Hawks said. "They got a lot of obsolete equipment."

He did not believe that the airship was Russian or German. But he might as well keep O'Brien from panicking now. Once the full truth was known, of course, O'Brien would have to go through an inevitable terror. Two Hawks hoped he could take it. He was having enough trouble quelling his own panic.

He sat up, yawned, stretched, and pretended an indifference he did not feel. The girl was sleeping near him; her lips were slightly open. Despite the dirt and the mosquito-repelling grease on her face, she looked cute. Like a pre-adolescent child who had been too tired to wash her face before going to bed. By now he knew her name, Huskarle Ilmika Thorrsstein. Huskarle, however, might be her title, corresponding to Lady. She was treated with great respect by the others.

She did not sleep very long, however. Dzikohses woke them all up, and they began walking in the daylight now. Apparently, he felt that they were far enough from the enemy to venture out under the sun. They saw very few farms after that, and the going became rougher. For several days the hills continued to get larger and the woods thicker. Then they were in the mountains. Two Hawks consulted his map. According to it, they should not yet be in the Carpathians. But they were here, and there was no use denying the reality of the mountains. Moreover, they seemed to him to be higher than the map indicated.

Their beef and bread and wine ran out. For a whole day, they walked along the lower slopes of the mountains without food. The next day, Ka'hnya, the bowman, slipped away into the forest while the others took a nap beneath the pines or birches. It was colder up here, and the nights were chilly enough to justify the heavy clothing they wore. Even so, the mosquitoes flourished during the day and part of the night. Somehow, they managed to find and to penetrate thin spots in the uniforms of Two Hawks and O'Brien, who could only complete escape by burying themselves under leaves.

Two hours later, Ka'hnya reappeared. He was a big man, but he was staggering under the weight of the half-grown boar on his shoulders. He smiled at the congratulations and rested while the others busied themselves butchering the giant porker. Two Hawks helped them, since he had had experience on his father's farm in such matters. He knew then that Dzikohses might consider their location safe enough for traveling in daylight, but he was not so confident that he wanted to risk firing a gun. Perhaps the bows and arrows had been brought along for just such safety measures. He did not think so. He got the impression from their odd assortment of weapons that these people had to use whatever was on hand. The two rifles with revolving chambers had probably been taken from dead enemies.

The pig was soon cooking over a number of small and relatively smokeless fires. Two Hawks ate hungrily and felt the strength flow back into him. The meat was strong and rank and only half-cooked, but he had no trouble wolfing it down. Ilmika Thorrsstein, however, seemed to have a delicate stomach. She refused the large chunk offered her. She smiled when she rejected it, but when she turned her face away and thought herself unseen, she could not repress a grimace of disgust. Then, as she watched the others eat, she seemed to have a change of mind—or of appetite. She took a small book from her bag and leafed through it. Two Hawks, looking over her shoulder, saw what appeared to be a calendar. It was not marked with Arabic numerals, however, but with numerals derived from the Greek alphabet. There were several that resembled runic symbols.

She asked Dzikohses a question. He came over and pointed at the second square in a row of seven figures. So, Two Hawks thought, they had a seven-day week. Ilmika smiled at this and said something to Dzikohses. He handed her the same piece he had offered before, and this time she ate.

Two Hawks could only deduce from this that pork was tabu for her except on certain days of the week.

"Curioser and curioser," he muttered.

O'Brien said, "What?" but Two Hawks did not answer. To try to explain the whole business would only confuse and perhaps frighten O'Brien. The sergeant looked too happy at the moment for Two Hawks to upset him further. Poor O'Brien unused to such long hard hikes and so little food, had been ready to keel over. Now he was even humming.

O'Brien patted his stomach, belched, and said, "Man, I feel great! If only I could get a week's sleep now, I'd be a new man; I could lick my weight in Kilkenny cats."

Several days later, they were still climbing along the lower parts of the mountains. Occasionally, they went higher to traverse a pass which would lead them down again. And then they were suddenly faced with a situation in which they had to use their firearms, noise or no noise. They had come down a mountain into a valley about six miles wide and twelve long. Part of the valley was wooded; the rest was a grassy plain and a marsh. Duck honks came from the marsh; a fox chased a hare not twenty feet in front of them. A big brown bear stood at the top of a small hill and watched them for a while before it turned and went back down the other side of the hill. The party crossed a band of trees splitting the valley in half and began to go across the wide plain. At that moment, they heard a loud bellow to their right. They whirled, their guns ready, and saw the great bull trotting towards them.

O'Brien, standing by Two Hawks, said, "Jesus, what a monster!"

The bull stood at least seven feet high at the shoulder; it was a glossy dark brown and had horns with a spread of at least ten feet.

"An aurochs!" Two Hawks said. He gripped his gun with the eery feeling that it was the only solid thing in the universe. He was not so frightened by the enormousness of the beast itself, since there was enough firepower in the group to knock down even this huge creature. What frightened him was that he felt as if he had been thrust back into the dawn of mankind. This was the kind of creature that early man had faced. Then he reassured himself that this was also a creature that man had wiped off the earth. Moreover, it, or something like it, was not so ancient after all. It had survived, though not in so great a form, up to and during World War I in the forests of Germany and Poland.

The aurochs bellowed and trotted towards them. Several times, it halted, threw up its head, and sniffed the air. Its black eyes gleamed in the sunlight, but whether it was pre-meditated murder or curiosity that shone there was not yet apparent. Fifty yards behind him, several cows thrust their lesser horned heads from behind bushes. Each of these looked large enough to take care of herself quite well, but they may have been hanging back to guard their calves. Two Hawks did not see any young and doubted that this was calving season. It did not matter whether or not the bull was protecting calves. His territory was being challenged, and he was intent on making sure that they intruded no longer.

Dzikohses said something to the men, then stepped out from them and shouted. The bull slowed down, stopped, and glared about him. Dzikohses shouted again. The aurochs wheeled and raced away and Two Hawks breathed easier. Then, as if driven by whim or as if he had caught a new scent which steered him around to face them again, he stopped and wheeled. The great head lowered; a huge hoof pawed the ground. Another vast bellow, and the bull was charging toward them. The ground trembled under the impact of hooves bearing a thousand pounds or more.

Dzikohses shouted more orders. His men spread out so that they could shoot at an angle at the aurochs and hit him in the body. The aurochs was not confused by this maneuver; he had evidently chosen the two Americans and Ilmika as his target. They had been standing in the center of the group and when the others went to left and right, they had stayed in the same spot as when they first saw the bull.

Two Hawks glanced at O'Brien and Ilmika and saw that they were not about to break and run. Ilmika was holding her revolver, its barrel resting on her left arm for steadiness.

O'Brien did not have a weapon, but he had taken a position just to the right of Two Hawks. He was poised to run.

"I'll go one way; you go the other," he said. "Maybe it won't know which one to take after."

By then the two muzzle-loaders and the rifles were firing. Ka'hnya loosed an arrow; it plunged into the right side of the beast just behind its shoulder. This did not stop it or even make it stagger. Though it shook at the impact of bullets and arrow, it kept on with unchecked speed. Ilmika began firing with no apparent effect. If her .40 caliber bullets struck the bull, they were hitting the thick bar of bone between the horns or glancing off the massive and tough neck muscles. Two Hawks told her to quit wasting her ammunition, but she did not even glance at him. Coolly, she kept on firing.

Then another arrow plunged into the bull, this time, whether by accident or design, into his right leg. He fell to one side and skidded on the grass, his inertia making him slide right up to Two Hawks feet. Two Hawks looked down at the great head and the enormous black eye glaring at him. The long eyelashes reminded him of a girl he had known in Syracuse—later he wondered why that irrelevant thought occurred to him in such a dangerous situation. Then he stepped up to put a bullet from the .32 through the eye. The other men closed in and shot into the body. It shuddered under the impact; by now blood was spurting from at least a dozen wounds. Nevertheless, so driving was its vitality, it started to rise again. Despite the crippling arrow in its leg, it managed to get onto all four legs.

Two Hawks placed the muzzle of his automatic only an inch from the eye—he had to raise the barrel upwards— and fired. The eye exploded and left an empty socket. In the midst of a roar, the auroch collapsed. He tried again to get up, then fell back on his side, gave a feeble bellow, and died.

Only then did Two Hawks start shaking. He thought he was going to get sick but the urge to upchuck died away and he was not forced to disgrace himself.

Dzikohses made sure that the bull was dead by cutting its throat. He arose with bloody knife and forgot about the bull for the time being. He looked all around the valley, worried that the sounds of the guns might bring unwelcome company. Two Hawks wanted to ask him whom he might expect to find in this remote place but decided against it. He not only was not sure that he would be understood; he thought it might be to his advantage if their captors thought they could speak freely in his presence. Actually, they were not too self-deluded. He comprehended only about one-sixteenth of what they said. But he was learning.

The men cut out pieces of meat from the flanks and rump. Ka'hnya started to slice away with the intention of getting to the heart. Dzikohses stopped him. The two argued for a moment, then Ka'hnya sullenly obeyed. From what he understood of the rapid conversation, Two Hawks deduced that Ka'hnya wanted the heart for more than its meat. Although he did not say so, he implied that they would all eat of the heart and so ingest the valor of the bull. Dzikohses would have none of this. He wanted to get across the plain and into the woods as swiftly as possible.

They traveled by wolf-trot: a hundred paces of fast trotting, a hundred of walking. They ate the miles up but at a price. By the time they reached the other end of the valley, where the woods and the mountain began, they were breathing heavily and soaked with sweat. Dzikohses was unmerciful. He began to climb at once. The rest of the party looked at each other and wondered if pleading for a rest would do any good or if it would be better to save their breath. Two Hawks grinned. He had his second wind by now and was determined to prove that he was as good a man as Dzikohses.

They had scrambled up the steep slope not more than fifty yards, going part of the way by pulling themselves up on the bushes, when a gun exploded nearby. Ka'hnya screamed and lost his hold and plunged backwards down the mountain. His head rammed into the base of a bush and stopped his descent. The rest of the party threw themselves down on the earth and looked around, but they saw nothing.

Then a gun barked again, and a bullet whistled through the leaves just over Two Hawks' head. He happened to be looking in the direction from which the fire came and saw the man lean halfway out from behind an oak. He did not try to answer the fire, since the shooter had popped back behind the tree. Moreover, at fifty yards, the automatic was too inaccurate. He might as well save his bullets.

Dzikohses called to them and began to worm towards the oaks just above him and to his left. The others followed him. Several times, guns exploded and bullets screamed above them or dug into the earth near them. By the sound, Two Hawks judged that their enemies were using muzzle-loaders. If so, they could not be too accurate at this range; Ka'hnya had been hit only because he was considerably exposed and motionless at the moment. Two Hawks decided to take a chance before the enemy could move in closer for a better shot. He jumped up and ran zigzag towards the oaks. No shots had come from that quarter. Either there were no hostiles there or else they were holding their fire. If the latter were true, then he was committing suicide, but there was only one way to find out.

Behind him and on both sides, shouts arose and guns boomed again. Bullets—or balls—ripped the air around him. He reached the oak with no near misses, although the missiles had come close enough to satisfy him. He waited, scanning the woods around him for a sight of anyone creeping close. He heard the thud of feet on the earth, and then Dzikohses was flying through the air and was down beside him. Two Hawks gestured at the big limbs above them. Dzikohses smiled, handed the rifle to Two Hawks and began climbing. On the lowest branch, he reached down and took the weapon back. He resumed climbing. Two Hawks followed him and stopped just below Dzikohses. Dzikohses was silent for a minute, then exclaimed with satisfaction. He aimed carefully, fired, and a man fell down from behind a tree. A moment later, he shot again. This time, a man began screaming. A third left the shelter of a bush to run crouching to the aid of the wounded man. Skehnaske', who probably was called The Fox because of his busy reddish hair, fired, and the running man spun around and then fell to the ground. He made the mistake of trying to get up; this time the entire party fired, and he was hurled backward by the force of several bullets.

There was silence for a while. Two Hawks saw some men dodge from one tree to another, apparently to meet behind a particularly large oak. Probably for a conference, he thought. Dzikohses did not try to shoot at them. He was waiting until he spotted somebody motionless and exposed.

He called to the others, and one by one they rose up and ran in a jagged path towards the oak. No shots were evoked by their flight. From his branch, Dzikohses gave directions to his men and also to the Huskarle Ilmika. They spread out on both sides of the oak and began working their way back down towards the mountain. Dzikohses stayed in the oak to send an occasional shot towards the tree that sheltered the enemy. Two Hawks followed Skehnaske' . O'Brien went with the

men on the left. For a while, Ilmika was with Skehnaske'
and Two Hawks, then she crawled off by herself.

Suddenly, a flurry of shots broke loose from the direction
of the tree which sheltered the enemy. Dzikohses answered,
firing as rapidly as possible. Two Hawks guessed that the
hostiles had abandoned the oak and were spreading out through
the woods for an ambush. He thought of how ironic it would be
if he were killed in this little skirmish in an isolated valley,
not knowing for whom he was fighting. For that matter, he
was not sure whom he was fighting with. Or why.

Ilmika's voice cried out to their right, succeeded by three
shots. Two came from muzzle-loaders; one, from a revolver.
Skehnaske' and Two Hawks went towards the place from
which the shots had come, but they proceeded cautiously,
taking advantage of every cover and pausing to reconnoiter.
Presently, they came upon a dead man, on his back, staring
upward, a hole torn out of his throat and blood over his
throat and chest. He wore a red handkerchief around his head,
his ears held large round silver rings, his long-sleeved shirt
had once been white. A purple cummerbund was around his
waist and in it was stuck a single-shot breech-loading pistol
and a long slim dagger. His trousers were baggy and knee-
length, and his coarse wollen stockings were black with scarlet
clockwork. His shoes were of a shiny black leather with
huge silver buckles.

The dead man's skin was as dark as that of a Hindu's.
He looked more like a gypsy than anything else.

The two separated and resumed their careful search. Although there were no signs of struggle, Two Hawks deduced
that the dead man's comrades had taken Ilmika prisoner. A
moment later, he saw the flash of a white shirt and then
Ilmika, her hands tied behind her, being shoved ahead by one
of her captors. The other, holding a six-shooter rifle, was a
few paces behind, alert for pursuers.

Two Hawks waited until they disappeared behind a rise
and then he circled to make sure he did not crawl into an
ambush. He heard faint cries, a slap, and the deep mutter of
men.

Something flashed to his left. He hugged the ground,
waited, and lifted his head cautiously. He saw Skehnaske'
signalling to him and signalled back. Then the red-haired
man crawled out of sight. Two Hawks wriggled like a snake
towards his targets, losing sight of them for a minute when

he went along a narrow trough formed by rainwater in the dirt. The rifle of Skehnaske' cracked; Two Hawks lifted his head to see the guard staggering backward but still holding on to his rifle. Two Hawks jumped up and shot at him within a range of twenty yards. Then he was running forward, only to hurl himself down behind a bush as the second man stood up briefly. The enemy fired at Two Hawks with a rifle, and his bullet thudded into the dirt only an inch from his face. Two Hawks rolled away towards a larger bush.

Skehnaske' kept on firing, and the enemy did not stick his head out again. Skehnaske' was shouting something at Two Hawks, who did not understand his words. Nevertheless, he got their meaning. He was up on his feet and rushed at the hillock while Skehnaske' resumed his covering fire. He tried to make as little sound as possible, but the man must have heard the slap of his shoes against the dirt. His black-handkerchiefed head appeared and then the barrel of his rifle. He was visible to Two Hawks but not to Skehnaske'. However, he was afraid to raise his head too high, and it was this that made his shooting awkward. He missed with the first bullet, swung the barrel around to correct, and fired again.

Two Hawks heard the bullet scream by. He was not surprised that he had not been hit, since he had seen Ilmika's feet kick out and slam into the man's ribs. The man froze for a second, unable to make up his mind to shoot at Two Hawks again or kill Ilmika. Two Hawks stopped and shot twice, both bullets hitting the man. One entered his right temple; the other struck him somewhere in the body. He collapsed, seeming to shrink like a balloon with a pinprick in it.

Ilmika wept and talked hysterically while Two Hawks untied her hands. They returned to the group, which had disposed of the others. Some of the enemy had gotten away; two were dead; one was taken alive with a bullet in his left thigh and another in his right shoulder. He squatted on the ground, his eyes dull with pain.

Dzikohses asked him some questions; the man spat at him. Dzikohses put the muzzle of his rifle against the man's temple and repeated the question. Again, the man spat. The rifle cracked. His head half-blown off, the man crashed into the ground.

Another wounded prisoner was brought in by Skehnaske'. Dzikohses was about to shoot him, too, then changed his mind. The prisoner was stripped of his clothes, his hands tied behind him, and his ankles bound together. He was hoisted up side down by a rope over a branch until his head was several feet off the ground. Dzikohses took the prisoner's own long thin dagger and cut off both ears. The man fainted. The party left him hanging there. Some time later, they heard him screaming, then silence came again. He must have passed out once more. A second time, they heard him screaming just as they passed over a shoulder of the mountain. After that, they heard him no more.

O'Brien and Two Hawks were both pale, but not from exertion. O'Brien said, "Mary preserve us! These gooks play rought!"

Two Hawks was watching the Lady Ilmika Thorrsstein. She seemed to have fully recovered. In fact, the incident of the tortured man had restored her color, and she seemed to have derived enjoyment from his punishment. He shuddered. Certainly, the gypsies, or whatever they were, would have done the same or worse to them if they had won. Yet he could never take vengeance in such a fashion. He would have had no compunction about shooting one in cold blood. But this! No, he might be an Iroquois Indian, but he was too civilized.

After that, he found that the blonde was not as aloof as she had been. She was grateful for his having rescued her, although the credit was only partly his. She talked with him whenever they had a chance and began to teach him her language. Now, though he wanted to learn her speech, he was the one who was constrained. It was a long time before he could forget the look on her face as she saw Dzikohses skewer the captive's ears.

5

Two WEEKS LATER, they came down out of the mountains. They were in very flat country and among farms. They were also near the enemy, the Perkunishans, as Ilmika called them. They resumed travel by night. Forty-eight hours later, they took refuge for the day in a huge house which had been the scene of a skirmish. Six bodies lay at various positions and distances from the house, and there were even more inside. The guerrillas had taken the house, but all had died in hand-to-hand fighting along with the Perkunishan soldiers holding it. No one was left to bury the dead, now overdue to be put into the earth. The party dragged the corpses out into a nearby copse of elms and laid them in two shallow graves. The muzzle-loaders were abandoned for the more modern six-shooters.

Two Hawks wondered why Dzikohses had not chosen a more hidden place for their rest. He listened to Dzikohses talk to some of his men—he was understanding at least half of the speech by now—and decided that this was a trysting place. Scouts came back to report that there were no hostiles in the neighborhood. However, cannon made thunder some miles away.

Two Hawks examined a big room which must have been the study of the master of the mansion. There were books on the shelves and on the floor, some destroyed by a bomb. A huge globe of Earth lay on the floor by the table from which it had been hurled by the explosion. He replaced it upright on the table. His heart beating hard, he verified his suspicions and cleared up some of the mysteries.

There were Asia, Africa, Europe, Australia, their outlines not quite those he had known. He spun the globe so it rotated eastward. The Pacific Ocean turned slowly by.

He sucked in his breath, aware that O'Brien, his jaw hanging down, was standing by him.

41

"What the hell?" O'Brien said, and then, "Mary, Mothe of Christ!"

There was Hawaii. Beyond it, a chain of islands startin where Alaska should be, running southeastward gently an ending in a large island where the plateau of Mexico shoul be. The Rockies and the Sierras. Rather, their islanded peaks A few dots in the east were the tops of the Alleghanies Everywhere else, water.

Central America was all blue. South America was anothe chain of islands, larger than those in the northern hemisphere the Andes.

Two Hawks, sweating more than the heat was responsibl for, studied the western hemisphere for a few minutes. The he spun the globe around to the eastern hemisphere. He ben over to read, or to try to read, the names printed thereon The alphabet, like that on Ilmika's calendar, was undoubtedl based on Greek. There was a familiar enough alpha and beta but the gamma faced to the left. And the digamma and koppa were still being used. Moreover, there were no capitals Rather, all the letters were capitals.

O'Brien groaned and said, "I'm going to throw up. I knev there was something wrong, but I couldn't put my finger o it. Where in hell are we?"

"Throwing up might make you feel better," Two Hawk said. "Afterwards, you'll have to face the truth just th same."

"Which is?"

"You ever read much science-fiction?"

"Naw. That goofy stuff."

"Better for you if you had. You might have a more flexibl mind. This situation might not be so hard for you to grasp Or to accept. Because, like it or not, you have to accept. O go crazy."

"I'm going crazy. Oh, my God, where's America? Where' Chicago?"

His voice was shrill. The others in the room stopped talk ing to look curiously at him.

"Ever heard of parallel universes?" Two Hawks said. " know you have because I've seen you read comic book that had just such a concept."

O'Brien looked relieved. "Yeah, I did. Only . . . hell you telling me we're in a parallel universe? A univers that's at right angles to ours?"

Two Hawks nodded and smiled at O'Brien's "right angles." This term was no explanation, only a method of description to make the reader better comprehend. Rather, make him think he was comprehending the incomprehensible. But if the term helped O'Brien get an anchor on reality, allayed his panic, he could keep it. Any anchor was better than none.

O'Brien said, "Then that funny feeling we got back in the *Hiawatha.* . . ? That was because we were going through a .. kind of a . . . gate?"

"You can call it a gate. The point is, the science-fiction fantasy has become for us a reality. There are parallel universes. I'd like to deny it just as much as you. But there's no denying this. Somehow, we've passed into another universe. We're on Earth, but not the one we knew."

O'Brien turned the globe to the western hemisphere. "And this Earth is one where North and South America are under water?"

He shivered and then crossed himself.

Two Hawks said, "I've known for some time that things that couldn't be nevertheless were. Those people"—he indicated the others in the room—"speak a language that is definitely Iroquoian."

He pointed at the blonde, Ilmika. "And her speech, believe it or not, is English. A species of English, anyway. She calls it *Ingwinetalu* or *Blodland spraech.*"

"You must be kidding? I thought she was a Swede or maybe a Dutchman. English?"

Two Hawks spun the globe back to the eastern hemisphere.

"On our Earth, the ancestors of the Amerind, the so-called American Indian, migrated in prehistoric times from Siberia to North America and on to South America. Group after group came over and may have taken over ten thousand years to do it. The Eskimo, the most Mongolian of what was essentially a Caucasian-Mongolian mixture, was the last to arrive.

"But on this Earth, the Amerind had no Americas to migrate to. So he turned inwards and became a force to reckon with in the Old World. That is, Asia and Europe."

He ran his finger over the map of Europe and stopped at the peninsula of Italy. The mauve color which overlay it extended through part of northern Yugoslavia and also covered Sicily. He read aloud the large title which evidently applied to the whole area.

"Akhaivia! Achaea? If Achaea, then the ancient Greeks

may have come down, for some reason, into the peninsula of what we call Italy in our world, instead of into the Hellenic peninsula!"

He looked at Greece. It was titled *Hatti*.

"Hittites?" he said aloud. "On our Earth, they conquered a part of Asia Minor, flourished for a while, contemporary with the Mycenaean Greeks, and then disappeared. What happened here? They invaded a country which the Greeks had bypassed, being shunted for some reason to the west. And the Hittites conquered the Pelasgians and gave their name to our Hellas?"

He continued talking aloud, partly to help O'Brien understand what had happened.

"I don't know the details and will have to guess at part of the outline. But I'll bet that the Iroquoians, and maybe other Amerind tribes, invaded eastern Europe and settled down. If they did so at an early date, they may have altered the course of the Indo-European migrations from the Motherland somewhere in Germany or Poland. The invasions resulted in bumping the various people—the Hittites, Hellenes, Italics, Germanics, and so forth—one country westward. Or something like that.

"Hmm! Wonder what happened to the Italics: the Sabines, Voluscans, Samnites, and the Latins? Were they bumped westwards? Or had they settled Italy before the Achaeans, only to be conquered and eventually absorbed by them?"

He placed his finger on a light green area covering approximately the area of Rumania and southern Russia. Hotinohsonih? House builders? Iroquoia? Sure! And that big cross there, Estokwa, would be our Earth's Odessa. Probably the capital of Hotinosonih. Estokwa? Paddle? It could be, though I don't know why a place would be named after a spatula or ladle. But then I don't know its history.

"I think we're headed for Estokwa, probably because the blonde, Ilmika Thorrsstein, is an important person. I've gathered from their conversation that her father was the Blodland ambassador to the nation of Dakota, our Hungary. Dakota? Could it be that Dakota is Siouian-speaking?"

He grinned and laughed and said to O'Brien, "Doesn't that make you feel a little more at home to know there's a state of Dakota here?"

He pointed at a river which ran from the north southward towards Estokwa and into the Black Sea. "This'll make you feel even more like home. Our Dnester is their 'Ohiyo', that is, 'a beautiful river'. And if I remember correctly, our Ohio River comes from an Iroquois word meaning beautiful. How's that strike you, O'Brien? Dakota and Ohio! Maybe things aren't so bad after all."

O'Brien smiled faintly and said, "Thanks for trying to cheer me up, Lieutenant. But it's going to take more than a couple of familiar names to get me over this shock. I still don't believe it."

Two Hawks said, "You might as well get with it." He pointed at a pale red area which covered approximately the Holland, Germany, Denmark, Poland, and Czechoslovakia of his world.

"Perkunisha. Sounds as if the word came from the Lithuanian Perkunis, the chief god of the ancient Lithuanians. And I've heard Dzikohses refer to the enemy as Pozosha. It could be his pronunciation of Borussia, another name for the Old Prussians who spoke a language related to Lithuanian."

He looked over the rest of the map of Europe (Eozope in Iroquoian). The northern half of the Scandinavian peninsula was in white—snow?—and a phantom polar bear was placed just above the lower border of the snowfield. He whistled and gave the globe a half-turn.

It was as he had suspected. The Gulf Stream was indicated. But, undiverted by the North American continent, which was sunk under the Atlantic, the Gulf Stream swung widely westward. It turned towards the west until it struck the cordillera of large and small islands formed by the unsubmerged parts of the Rockies. It traveled parallel with the string of islands and then met the Japanese current.

He whistled again. Here was a factor far more significant in the history of this world's Europe than the presence of the Amerindian.

He said, "It's hot here now. But I bet it doesn't last long, and it'll be a hell of a long cold winter."

Two Hawks went to the shelves and looked through several books. He found an atlas with more detailed maps than the globe. Moreover, the accompanying text and the titles on the maps were bilingual, Greek and Iroquoian. The Greek was difficult for him, since it varied from the Homeric and Attic and also seemed to have loanwords from languages totally alien to him. But he could read it easier than he could the Iroquoian.

He spoke to O'Brien, who was looking over his shoulder. "I wondered why I saw no horses. What's more, we're not going to find any camels in this world. Nor tobacco, tomatoes, turkeys, and I could go on and on."

"How come?"

"Horses, the horses we knew on our Earth, orginiated on the North American continent. Then they spread to the Old World, only to become extinct later on in the Americas. They were reintroduced there by the Spaniards. The camel family had its genesis in America, too. It traveled to Asia, and in America most of the species died out, except for the llama, alpaca, and guanaco. And now you know why nobody knew what you wanted when you tried to borrow a cigarette."

"Hey!" O'Brien said. "Rubber! That's why those armored cars were traveling on wood-and-iron wheels. No rubber!"

"You won't be able to eat chocolate here, either."

"What a hell of a world!" O'Brien said. "What a hell of a world!"

"We're here. We might as well make the best of it."

He stopped talking because a number of strangers had come into the room. There were twenty, most of them dark-skinned and dark-haired, but a few had coloring pale as O'Brien's. They were in light green uniforms and brown leather knee-length boots. Their trousers were skin-tight and piped with gold thread along the seam. The coats were swallow-tailed, loose around the chest and sleeves with, four large button-down pockets. Their helmets were conical, like Chinese coolie hats but curving downward in back to protect the neck. The officers wore symbolic feathers of steel affixed to the helmet front. All carried breech-loading single-shot rifles and slightly curving swords about four feet long. All were beardless.

Their commanding officer talked for a while with Dzikohses. He looked frequently at the Americans. The officer, a kidziaskos (from the Greek *chiliarchos*), suddenly frowned. He left Dzikohses and strode to the fliers. He demanded that Two Hawks hand over his gun. Two Hawks hesitated, then shrugged. He had to comply. After making sure that the safety of the automatic was on, he handed the gun to the officer. The kidziaskos turned it over and over and finally stuck it in his belt.

Dzikohses and his guerrillas left; the fliers and Ilmika Thorrsstein were escorted from the house by the soldiers.

Again, they marched by night and slept as well as they could during the day. Apparently, the enemy had overrun this area but did not have a tight control as yet. The party avoided all Perkunishan patrols but could not get away from the swarms of huge mosquitoes. All were forced to apply a thick coating of the stinking grease every day.

Two days after they had separated from the guerrillas, O'Brien began to suffer from chills, fever, and sweating. Two Hawks thought the sergeant had malaria. The medico with the troops confirmed his diagnosis.

"For God's sakes, don't they have any quinine?" O'Brien said. "You'd think that in a country where they have malaria, they'd . . ."

"There isn't any," Two Hawks said. "It was unknown on our Earth until after South America was discovered. So . . ."

"What'd they do before Columbus? They must've had something!"

"I don't know. Whatever they had, it wasn't very effective."

He did not tell O'Brien that malaria had been a great killer in the Mediterranean region of their Earth. In fact, it still took a large annual toll. He was worried, not only for O'Brien but for himself. The malaria parasite could kill a man if he got no medical aid, especially since the parasite of this world might be even more deadly than those of his.

The soldiers made a rude stretcher from two branches and a blanket. The sergeant was placed on it; Two Hawks took one end of the stretcher and a soldier the other. The troops relieved each other at fifteen-minute intervals, but Two Hawks had to stay at his task until his hands could lock themselves around the branches no more, his legs were like stone, and his back felt as if it would unhinge at the next step.

The medico gave O'Brien water and two large pills, one red, one green, every hour. Whatever the ingredients, they had little effect. O'Brien continued to chill, burn, and sweat in turn for four hours. Then the attacks ceased, as could be expected. Although he was weak, he was forced to rise and walk, with Two Hawks supporting him. The officer made it plain that he wanted no lagging. Two Hawks urged O'Brien to keep going. The officer would have no compunctions about killing a possible spy who was holding them up. His main concern evidently was in getting the Blodland woman through the enemy and to the capital city.

After four days of travel, during which O'Brien became

sicker and weaker, they came to their first village. They walked during the daytime hours the last 12 hours. The enemy must not have advanced very near to this point. Here Two Hawks saw the first railroad and locomotive. The locomotive looked like an engine circa 1890, except that the huge smokestack was shaped like a demon's face. The cars of the train were painted scarlet and covered with good luck signs, including the swastika.

The village was the terminus for the line. Thirty houses and stores were parallel with both sides of the tracks. Two Hawks gazed curiously at the houses and the people who ran out to greet them. The buildings reminded him of the false-fronted structures seen in Western movies. However, each had a wooden and brightly painted carving of a tutelary spirit in front of it and also one like a ship's figurehead near the top of the false front. The men wore heavy boots and shirts of cloth or cowhide or deerskin. The shirts hung outside their belts. The women wore bead-fringed, low-cut blouses of cloth and ankle-length skirts. Small stone carvings or sea shells were sewn in various patterns on the skirts. Both sexes had long hair falling to the shoulders; the German-helmet haircuts of the guerrillas and the soldiers, Two Hawks thought, must be military requirements.

There were a few old men and women, all of whose faces and hands were tattooed in blue and red. He supposed that this skin decoration had been a universal custom among the Hotinosonih. Something, possibly the influence of the white West European nations, had caused the tattooing to die out.

The officer politely asked the Thorrsstein woman to step aboard a passenger car. He was not so polite to the two Americans. He shouted at them to go three cars back. Two Hawks pretended not to understand, since he did not want his captors to know he was gaining fluency in their tongue. Some soldiers shoved the two toward the car. Two Hawks, assisting the chattering shaking sergeant, went up the steps and into the mobile prison.

The car was bare of furniture and crowded with wounded soldiers. Two Hawks found a place for O'Brien to stretch out on the wooden floor. Then he looked for water for O'Brien, but discovered that it was available only in the next car. A man with an arm in a bloody sling and a bloody bandage around his head accompanied Two Hawks. The wounded man held a long knife in his good hand and promised to cut Two

Hawks' throat if he so much as looked like he meant to escape. He did not leave the side of the prisoners during the rest of the long trip to 'Estokwa.

This took five days and nights. Many times, the train was shifted to a sidetrack to allow trains loaded with soldiers to pass westwards. During one day, nobody in the hospital car had water. O'Brien almost died that day. But the train finally stopped near a creek, and the bottles and canteens were refilled.

The car was jammed, hot, noisy, and malodorous. A man with a badly gangrened leg lay next to the sergeant. His stench was so nauseating that Two Hawks could not eat. The third day, the soldier died and was buried four hours later in the woods near the tracks while the locomotive puffed impatiently on a spur.

Surprisingly, O'Brien improved. By the time they got to 'Estokwa, the fever, chill, and sweating were gone. He was pale, weak, and gaunt, but he had beaten his sickness. Two Hawks did not know whether the recovery was due to the Irishman's basic toughness, the pills which the medico had continued to dose him with, or a combination of the two. It was also possible that he had been afflicted with something besides malaria. It did not matter; he had health again, even if only a precarious one.

6

THE NIGHT THE TRAIN arrived in 'Estokwa, a rainstorm was lashing the city. Two Hawks could see nothing through the windows except lightning flashes, nor was he allowed to get a better look after being escorted off the car. His eyes were bound, his hands tied behind him, and he was taken through the rain to a wagon. He knew it was enclosed because he could hear the water fall on the roof, and his back was up against a wall. He sat on a bench on one side of the cabin and O'Brien, also blindfolded, sat on the other.

"Where do you think they're taking us, lieutenant?"

O'Brien sounded weak and nervous. Two Hawks replied that he did not know. Privately, he supposed that they were being taken to an interrogation station. He hoped fervently that civilization had softened the old Iroquois methods of dealing with prisoners. Not that being "civilized" necessarily meant that subtle or brutal torture was out of consideration. Look at the "civilized" Germans of his own world. Look at the Russians. Look at the Chinese. Look at the American whites in their dealings with the red man. Look at anybody, preliterate or civilized.

After an estimated fifteen minutes of travel, the wagon stopped. O'Brien and Two Hawks were roughly helped down. Ropes were put around their necks, and they were led up a long flight of steps, down a long hall, down another, then down a curving staircase. Two Hawks said nothing; O'Brien cursed. Abruptly, they were halted. A door swung open on squeaky iron hinges; they were pushed through a doorway. Again halted, they stood in silence for a while. Their blindfolds were removed, and they were blinking at the bright illumination of an electric lamp.

When his vision had come back, Two Hawks saw that the room was of polished granite. Its ceiling was far above; the light came from a huge lamp on a wooden table. Several men stood around them. These wore tight-fitting black uniforms; on the left breast of each jacket was a misshapen death's head. And, unlike any he had seen so far, these men had completely shaven heads.

He had been right. He and O'Brien were here to be interrogated. Unfortunately, they really had nothing to tell. The truth was so incredible that the questioners would not believe it. They would think that it was a fantasy concocted by Perkunishan spies. They could not think otherwise, any more than a man of this world, caught in a similar situation in Two Hawks' Earth, would be believed by either Allies or Germans.

Nevertheless, there came a time when Two Hawks told the truth, unbelievable or not. O'Brien was the lucky one. Weakened by the malaria, he could not endure much pain. He kept fainting until the inquisitioners were satisfied that he was not faking. They dragged him out by his heels, his head bobbling on the smooth greasy-looking stone. Then they devoted their full energies and ingenuity to Two Hawks. Perhaps they were especially vindictive because they believed him to be a traitor. He was obviously not a Perkunishan.

Two Hawks kept silent as long as possible. He remembered that the old Iroquois of his Earth had admired a man who could take it. Sometimes, though rarely, they stopped the torture to adopt a man of great courage and endurance into the tribe.

After a while he began wondering how his ancestors could have been so tough as to keep silent, even to sing and dance or yell insults at their tormentors. They were better men than he. To hell with the stoicism and with the defiance! He began to scream. This did not make him feel better, but it at least permitted him some expression and release of energy.

The time came when he had babbled his story five times, insisting each time that it was true. Six times he fainted and was revived with ice-cold water poured over him. After a while, he did not know what he was doing or saying. But at least he was not begging for mercy. And he was cursing them, telling them what low worthless despicable creatures they were and vowing to cut their guts out and loop them around their necks when he got a chance.

Then he began screaming again, the world was one red flame, one red scream.

When he awoke, he was in pain. But it was more like the

memory of pain. The memory hurt enough but was far pref-
erable to the actual agony inflicted on him in that stone
chamber. Still, he wished he could die and get the exquisite
hurt over with. Then he thought of the men who had done this
thing to him, and he wished he would live. Once on his feet,
give him a chance to escape, and he would somehow kill them.

Time passed. He awoke to find his head being held up
and a cooling drink going down his dry throat. There were
several women in the room, all clad in long black robes and
with white bands around their foreheads. They shushed his
croaked questions and began to change some of the bandages
in which he was swathed. They did so gently but could not
avoid hurting him. Afterwards, they applied soothing lotions
and put fresh bandages on.

He asked where he was, and one answered that he was in
a nice safe place and no one was ever going to hurt him again.
He broke down and cried then. They looked to one side as if
embarrassed, but he did not know if they were embarrassed
by the show of emotion or by what had been done to him.

He did not stay awake long but fell into a sleep from
which he awoke two days later. He felt as if he had been
drugged; his head was as thick as the taste in his mouth. He
managed to get out of bed that evening and to walk up and
down the long hall outside his room. Nobody interfered, and
he even talked—or tried to talk—to some of the other patients.
Shocked, he returned to his tiny room. O'Brien was in the
other bed. Weakly, O'Brien said, "Where are we?"

"In the Iroquoian version of the booby hatch," Two Hawks
said.

O'Brien was too drained of strength to react violently. He
did succeed in talking, however. "How come we're here?"

"I suppose our torturers, the Iroquois Gestapo, concluded
we had to be insane. We stuck to our story, and our story
could not possibly be true. So, here we are, and lucky at that.
These people seem to have preserved the old respect for
the crazed. They treat them nicely. Only, we're prisoners, of
course."

O'Brien said, "I don't think I'm going to make it. I think
I'm going to die. What they did to me . . . and being on
this world, I . . ."

"You're too mean and ornery to die," Two Hawks said.
"Where's your fighting Irish spirit? You tough mick, you'll
make it all right. You just want some sympathy."

"No. But promise me one thing. When you get the chance, find those bastards and kill them. Slowly. Make them scream like they made us scream. Then kill them!"

Two Hawks said, "I felt like you did. But I've discovered something about this world. There aren't any Geneva conventions. What happened to us happens to any prisoner if the captors feel like torturing him. If we'd fallen into the hands of the Perkunishans, we'd have gotten the same treatment or worse. At least, we aren't crippled for life or permanently scarred. From now on, we've got it made. We're being treated like kings. Like captive gods. The Iroquois regard the insane as possessed by divinity. Maybe they don't really believe that any more, but the basic attitude still exists."

"Kill them!" O'Brien said, and he fell asleep again.

By the end of the following week, Two Hawks was almost back to normal. The third-degree burns were still healing, but he no longer felt as if he had been flayed alive and every exposed muscle and nerve beaten in a mortar. He met the director of the asylum, Tarhe. Tarhe was a tall thin man with a huge nose and the eyes of a gentle eagle. In addition to being the chief administrator, he was also the head *latoolats.* This word meant, literally, *he hunts,* and was the generic term for the Iroquoian equivalent of psychiatrist.

Tarhe was a kindly man and a scholar. He gave Two Hawks permission to use his library, in which Two Hawks spent hours each day learning about this world, or Earth 2, as he was beginning to call it. There were books in every major language and many in the minor tongues and over a hundred volumes of reference material. There was also a multilingual dictionary which Two Hawks used frequently. His education leaped ahead like a hare with a fox on its trail.

Occasionally, Tarhe called him in for brief therapeutic sessions. Tarhe was a busy man, but he considered Two Hawks' case a challenge. As time went on, he allotted an hour a day to his patient, although for Tarhe it meant losing an hour of sleep or of study for himself.

"Then you think that I had some experience on the western front that was so terrible that my mind snapped?" Two Hawks said. "I retreated from reality into the fantasy world of this Earth I claim to be from? I found this world unendurable?"

Two Hawks grinned at Tarhe and said, "If that is true, why would O'Brien have exactly the same psychosis? The same down to every minute detail? Don't you find it strange. indeed incredible, that we could agree on a thousand details of this fantasy world?"

Tarhe said, "He found your psychosis attractive enough to want to get into it. No wonder. He obviously depends upon you a great deal; he would feel shut out, absolutely alone, if he were not in this . . . this Earth 1."

Tarhe did not use the term psychosis or anything like it. His word, translated literally, meant "possession." It was used because a *latoolats* treated the insane as if they were actually possessed by a demon or an evil ghost. The demons, however, were dealt with scientifically; they had been categorized. One of Tarhe's medical books gave a list of one hundred and twenty-nine types of evil spirits. Two Hawks was supposed to have been taken over by a *teotya'tya'koh* (literally, *his body is cut in two*).

Suspecting that Tarhe was too intelligent and too basically incredulous to believe in the existence of ghosts and demons, Two Hawks questioned him. Tarhe replied with a smile and some carefully chosen ambiguous phrases. They satisfied Two Hawks that Tarhe used the terms only to conform to the scientific terminology of his profession. There may have been a time when the categorizations were literal and not figurative, but men like Tarhe no longer put credence in them. However, the belief in demons was a living force among the common people and the priests of the state religion. It might be dangerous to publicly profess disbelief. So, Tarhe went along with public opinion.

The amazing thing was that the principles of treating the mentally sick were much the same as those used by the Freudian practicioners of Earth 1. The Iroquoian explanations for the genesis and cure of warped minds might be different, but the therapy was similar.

"How do you account for our ignorance of your language?" Two Hawks said to Tarhe.

"You're an intelligent man. Your *teotya'tya'koh* is cunning. It decided to go all the way into this dream world. So it made you forget your native tongue. Thus, you are even more secure from being forced back into this world."

"You have a rationalization for everything I say," Two Hawks said. "In fact, you rationalize so much, one might think you were the patient and I the doctor. Have you ever considered, even for one second, that I might be telling the truth? Why not conduct an experiment to determine this; take a truly scientific nonprejudicial approach? Question O'Brien and myself separately about our world. We could have agreed on a story in its broad outlines. But if you delve into it, break it down to very minor details—oh, about a thousand things: language, history, geography, religions, customs, etcetera—you'll find an absolutely astonishing agreement."

Tarhe removed his glasses and polished them.

"That would be a scientific experiment. It's true you couldn't create an entire language in all its complexities of sound, structure, vocabularly, and so forth. Or agree on details of history, architecture, and so on."

"So why don't you test us?"

Tarhe replaced his glasses and looked owlishly at Two Hawks.

"Some day, I may. Meanwhile, let's work on your possession, find out how the demon managed to invade you. Now, what were your feelings—not thoughts—when I contradicted you a moment ago?"

Two Hawks was furious at first, then he began to laugh. After all, he could not blame Tarhe for his attitude. If he were in his place, would he believe such a story?

Much of Two Hawks' time was taken up with the routine of the asylum. There were the daily sweatbaths, so long and hot that if a demon were inhabiting his body, it would have been too uncomfortable to remain. There were daily religious ceremonies, during which the priests from a nearby temple tried to exorcise the demons. Tarhe absented himself during these; apparently, he had had trouble concealing his impatience with priests. He must have felt that they were wasting time that could be better spent. It was an indication of the power of the Iroquois church that he dared not interfere with it. Two Hawks made some inquiry about the state religion and found that it was indigenous. It was based on the primitive religions of the Iroquois and had been formalized and put into writing some four hundred years ago by a prophet, Kaasyotyeetha'. The founder of the religion had made the vaguely pantheistic belief into a monotheistic one. And he had incorporated various concepts and creeds of the Western European religion into the new faith. However, all the borrowings had an Iroquoian flavor.

There was, however, religious toleration in the nation of Hotinohsonih.

In his leisure time, Two Hawks went to the library or practised conversation with the patients and staff. He intended to escape some day and would thus have to know this world well if he were to operate effectively. A children's book, printed by a house in 'Estokwa, gave him an outline of Earth 2's prehistory and history. The planet was now in the terminal stage of an ice age, just entering a warm period. This was a good thing for Europe, otherwise all of the northern half and part of the southern would be under a permanent icecap. The lack of a Gulf Stream to heat up the continental climate had made a big difference in man's technological development and in his expansion. A good part of the Scandinavian peninsula and of northern Russia was icebound most of the year. The lack of horse and camel also seemed to have slowed man's travel and communication.

Over the course of several thousand years, large migrations of Amerinds (generally referred to by Westerners as anthropophagi) from central Asia and Siberia had wandered into Europe and conquered or been conquered. The conquerers had usually been absorbed into the defeated peoples, who had then regained their national identity and integrity.

But in fairly recent times, during the past 800 years, several of the later invaders had succeeded in imposing their language and some cultural traits on the white aborigines. The area of Czechoslovakia of Earth 1 was here called Kinukkinuk. The Algonquian word for this state had originally meant *mixture* and had referred both to the differing dialects of the various conquerors and also to the fact that the Amerinds had miscegenated with the white natives.

This reminded Two Hawks of Hungary of Earth 1, where a semi-Mongolian people, speaking a Uralic tongue, had defeated the whites, imposed their language upon the whites, and then had been absorbed, losing their racial identity. Here, the Huns had never been heard of.

The Finnish speakers had been diverted eastwards, invaded and settled down in Japan, known on Earth 2 as Saariset. The Japanese, repelled when they had tried to conquer the islands, had turned instead to the area of what Two Hawks' planet knew as southern China. Northern China was inhabited by a Mongolian-type people speaking an Athabaskan tongue similar to Navaho and Apache.

India, Burma, Malaya, and Indonesia were similar to the countries of Earth 1. But there were differences. Some of the

rthern Indian rajahdoms spoke Turkic, and Arabic was
evalent in the southern part.

Asia Minor presented an alien picture. The Turkey of
arth 1 spoke Hittite. Palestine used a Semitic tongue derived
om colonists from Crete. Hebrew was unknown. The rest
: Asia Minor, except for Arabia, spoke Indo-Iranian dia-
cts.

The Akhaiwoi (a Hellenic tribe) had conquered the
alic peninsula and given it its present name of Akhaivia.
hey had built up a civilization that could be compared
vorably in some respects to the Athenian culture of Earth
although lacking in others.

Egypt had its own Greek dialect. The other North African
ates spoke Berber, Iberian, or Greek. Unlike the semidesert
orth Africa of Earth 1, these nations had very fertile soil
d a large population.

The Germanic peoples had begun invading Britain and
eland at an early date. Succeeding waves of Germanics,
eltics, and even Baltics came so fast and furious that Britain
came known as Blodland (Bloodland). The Ingwine
ally established themselves in Blodland, and their speech
veloped into something like the Old English of Earth 1. But
en the Danish and Norwegian raids and invasions began.
ney were on a scale that far surpassed those of Earth 1. In
ct, half of Denmark migrated to Blodland over a period of
hundred years and settled down there.

Danish kings ruled for a long time. Under them, Iceland,
eland, Norland (Scotland), Blodland, Grettirsland (Nor-
andy), and south Scandinavia became known as the Six King-
ms and had remained so until modern times. All of the
states spoke dialects of a common language, Ingwinetalu.
is could be described as an archaic and creolized English
th an enormous stock of Norse loanwords and a lesser
ount of Semitic Cretan, Etruscan Rasna, and Greek loan-
rds.

The French and Latin words were missing, and oh, what a
ference their lack made to the language! Learning Ingwin-
was for Two Hawks learning a foreign tongue.

Perkunisha, the Baltic-speaking nation, consisted of Earth
Germany, Holland, Denmark, Poland, and the Algon-
ian speakers of Earth 1's Czechoslovakia, Kinukkinuk.

The Perkunishans seemed to be the Germans of Earth 2
far as their industry, science, philosophy, and aggressive-

ness were concerned. Thirty years ago they had begun th
planet's first World War I. They had seemed on their way
the complete conquest of Europe and North Africa when
plague (the Black Plague?) had decimated Europe. Nov
their armies powerful with a new generation and a militaril
superior technology and a superman ideology, the Perkunishar
were trying again. This time, it looked as if they mig
succeed.

Two Hawks saw what a difference the lack of a Unite
States of America made in this world. Europe could n
call upon them for aid against the Central European aggressor

7

ERGEANT O'BRIEN, despite his convictions that he was going
o die, got better. Soon he was on his feet and doing simple
xercises. Two Hawks was working out with him in the
ymnasium one day when an orderly told him he had a visitor.
wo Hawks felt apprehensive, wondering if the secret police
ad come for him. He followed the orderly to the visitors'
oom. He was ready to kill if he had to and then to make an
scape. If he was killed instead, so much the better. He was
ot going through that torture again.

On entering the room, his grimness dissolved into a smile.
he Lady Ilmika Thorrsstein was waiting for him. She con-
nued to sit in her chair, as befitted a member of the Blod-
and nobility in the presence of a commoner. However, she
id reply to his smile with one of her own.

Two Hawks kissed her extended hand and said, "Ur Hus-
arleship (Your Ladyship)."

"Hu far't vi thi, lautni Tva Havoken?" she said. ("How
oes it with you, freeman (or Mister) Two Hawks?")

"Ik ar farn be'er," he said. ("I am doing better.") "Ur
Iuskarleship ar mest hunlich aeksen min haelth of." ("Your
Ladyship is most gracious in asking about my health.")

She certainly gave no hint of having recently gone through
n ordeal. She was no longer the dirty, hollow-cheeked,
atigue-eyed and smelly woman he had known on the
ight through the forest. She had put on some weight, rounded
ut nicely, and her eyes were clear, the dark circles gone.
Ier lips were roughed a dark red, her face was slightly
owdered, and her cheeks lightly rouged. She wore one of the
all conical hats from which hung a thin blue gauze strip, the
vhole reminding him of the hats worn by the ladies of me-
lieval times. Her dress was of some shiny pale white stuff, form
'tting from the waist up, cut low and square at the bosom.
\ ruff of yellow lace circled her waist, and the skirt, held out

by several stiff petticoats, fell to her ankles to shape truncated cone. Her high-heeled shoes were of white leathe and bore tiny blue puffballs on the toes.

She was very pretty. Two Hawks, looking at her, suddenl felt the thrust of desire that had been too long subdued b the rigors of the flight and then by the torture. Returnin strength and long abstinence was making him extraordinaril horny, he thought. Or maybe not so extraordinarily. Just hi usual state.

But this woman was not for him. He had learned of th strong class barriers that existed throughout most of Europe They were as rigidly and harshly enforced, perhaps even mor so, than they had been in, say, seventeenth-century France.

Only the country of the Hotinohsonih—"his people"— had anything approaching the American concept of democracy This was the only nation which had given its women the righ to vote. He was from a world and a time which regarded th social barriers of this world as of little importance, even ridic ulous. So he could not help looking boldly at her. Some of hi desire must have shown, for she lost her smile, and her eye narrowed. He hastened to reassure her, since he did not wisl to offend her and so lose his only personal contact with th outside world.

"Foryi me, faeyer Huskarle," he said. "Ik n'a seen sw bricht a faemme for maniy a daey. Yemiltsa." ("Forgive me fair lady. I have not seen so bright a maiden for many day. Show mercy.")

He added with a smile, "Besides, I am not responsibl for my actions. Otherwise, I would not be here."

She smiled, though strainedly, and said, "You are forgiven And I am happy that you brought up the subject of you . . . uh . . . staying here."

"Call it imprisonment," he said. "Although I can't com plain about my treatment. They're very nice."

She leaned forward and said, face intent, "I don't thinl you're crazy."

He was a little startled and then it occurred to him tha she had been left alone with him. That would not have bee done unless she had requested it, since she was an importan person. He had learned that she was the daughter of Huskarl that is, Lord, Thorrsstein, the Blodland ambassador to th nation of Dakota. Thorrsstein and his daughter had fled to wards Iroquoia when the Perkunishans invaded Dakota. Th

Lord and his daughter had become separated, and later Ilmika had been taken by guerrillas through the Perkunishan lines.

"What makes you think I'm not mad?" he said. He knew now that she was not here merely to make a social call.

"I just cannot believe it," she replied. Making an effort to hide her tension, she sat back in the chair. She folded her hands on her lap and said, "If you are not crazy, then what are you?"

He decided he could not lose by telling her the truth. If she had been sent by the secret police to see if he gave her a different story, she would return with the same they had heard. However, it was not likely that the Hotinohsonih had asked her to probe for them. They would have gotten verification from Tarhe that Two Hawks was sticking to his tale.

More probably, Ilmika represented her own people, the Blodland secret agents. Perhaps they had information which the Hotinohsonih lacked. This information might have made them think that Two Hawks could be from a "parallel" universe and so had knowledge of a superior technology. The wreck of the *Hiawatha* could have been discovered. If it had been, it would present the finders with a disturbing puzzle. The Blodland agents, knowing of it and also of the two strangers and their story, had contacted Lady Thorrsstein. She was to question him to determine if he could be useful.

If this were the true situation, the Blodlandish were not telling their Hotinohsonih allies what they knew. The Blodlandish wanted the information for themselves.

He smiled. Even in the desperate predicament in which both allies were, one was playing against the other. Power politics and national security were as paramount here as on his Earth.

Still, the Blodlandish interest gave him a bargaining position. It might permit O'Brien and himself to escape not only from the asylum but from a country that seemed to be on it way to being defeated and occupied. So far, Blodland was not threatened by invasion.

Before starting his narrative, Two Hawks explained the concept of "parallel" universes as best he could. Ilmika listened attentively, and her questions showed that she was as intelligent as she was pretty. She had no difficulty in understanding him, but whether or not she believed him was another matter. Nevertheless, she encouraged him to go on, which meant she was willing to grant the possibility he might not

be a lunatic. Or perhaps she had been told to get his entire
story, even if it sounded to her like ravings.

Two Hawks followed his "theory" with a broad outline of
how his Earth differed from her *Erthe,* as it was called in
Blodlandish. Then he gave her the background of World War
II and of his involvement. He ended with a description of
the great American bombing raid on Ploesti and the passing
of the *Hiawatha* through the "gate" and the parachuting into
the peasant's field.

"Your Ploesti is *Tkanotaye'koowaah* or, as it's called in
Western Europe, Dares, after the original Trojan name," she
said. "The Perkunishans wanted it for the same reason your
Germans wanted its counterpart. Oil and gas. You were fortunate you arrived when you did. One day later, and you
would have fallen into the enemy hands. They had the area
under complete control by then."

Two Hawks walked to the huge picture window which gave
a view of 'Estokwa. The asylum was on a high hill a few
miles from the center of the capitol. The great white marble
building of the *Teyotoedzayashohkwa',* the Iroquoian version
of Parliament or of Congress, dominated the metropolis. To
one side was a smaller building, also in Greek style but of
red granite. This was the residence of the *hakya'tanoh*
(literally, *he watches over me*), the elected chief executive.

'Estokwa, once a seaport of the Trojan colonists, had
been razed and its inhabitants massacred when the Iroquoians
had taken it after a long siege. The longhouses of the bar-
barians had been built in the midst of the stone ruins. But now
'Estokwa was a modern city, indistinguishable at a distance
from most West European metropolises. The government
and business buildings were constructed of marble or granite
and modeled after the classical Akhaivian architecture.

Two Hawks had seen closeup photos of the congressional
building in Tarhe's office. The pillars of the great portico
were carved to represent the seven tutelary animals of the
seven major tribes that 'had comprised the original invaders.
The exterior walls were covered with friezes depicting not
only scenes from history but weird symbolic figures repre-
senting characters from religion and folklore. These were
executed in the distinctive non-European style that the "red
men" had developed after becoming civilized.

Two Hawks wanted it to be otherwise, but he had no genuine identification with these people. They were "Iroquois,"

but not the Iroquois he knew. Their past, and present, were too dissimilar, and the influences under which they had come were also too alien. He actually had less identification with them than he had with the white culture of his native United States of America.

Given time, he might have made a satisfactory adjustment. But this nation seemed destined to go down into defeat under the overwhelming might of Perkunisha. If it did, it would give him no home. It would be a hell. The official policy of Perkunisha towards conquered nations was the absolute destruction of all non-Perkunishan traits. First, genocide on a scale that not even the Germany of his world had been bold enough to proclaim publicly. Then colonization by Perkunishans and other Europeans thought sufficiently Nordic to be given Perkunishan citizenship.

Even now, a battle was raging some twenty miles to the west and north of 'Estokwa. Three enemy armies were battering steadily towards the gates of the capitol. Unless something unlikely happened, the invaders would be in 'Estokwa within a week. There would be house-to-house fighting then, but the government itself was making plans to evacuate.

As he looked over the city, he saw three dots appear in the blue sky. Presently, they were close enough to be seen as dirigibles. Three huge silvery cigar-shapes, they slid through the air while little black puffs of smoke arose beneath them. Serenely, they ignored the futile and primitive anti-aircraft fire and proceeded towards their targets, the congressional building and chief executive's residence. Many little objects fell from the mammoths' bellies as they passed one by one over the targets. Clouds of smoke with hearts of fire pillared up from the ground. A few seconds later, the picture window rattled, the asylum building trembled, and he heard the not-too-far-off boom, boom, boom.

Other great sausages appeared. More bombs. The hemispherical roof of the legislators' building was gone. Wooden houses began to blaze. A factory went up in smoke and flying beams.

Two Hawks heard a door open behind him in one of the brief recesses between the explosions of bombs. He turned to see Thorrsstein's slave stick her head inside the room. She was a pretty girl of Amerind-white ancestry, a descendant of the aboriginal whites enslaved by the Hotinohsonih. The lady Thorrsstein had mentioned earlier that the girl had

been loaned to her by the Hotinohsonih government becaus
she could speak Blodlandish. Normally, she was stationed a
the Blodland embassy in 'Estokwa. Probably, she was a sp
for the Hotinohsonih.

Ilmika asked what she wanted. The girl timidly replie
that she wanted to make sure her mistress was all right, tha
she was not distressed by the bombing. Ilmika did look pale
and her back was even more rigid than usual. But sh
managed to smile and to say that she was quite all right
thank you. The slave girl remained in the room until ordere
to leave. Not until the girl had closed the door behind he
did Ilmika speak again. By that, Two Hawks knew that she to
suspected the girl. That must also be why Ilmika had permit
ted herself to be alone in a room with a man. Custom de
manded that any unmarried woman of noble birth always b
chaperoned under such situations.

Ilmika spoke in a low voice. "My government has reaso
to believe that your story could be true."

"They know of the flying machine," he said.

"Yes. But there is more. Perkunisha knows of it, also
Moreover, they have another flying machine. They also hav
the man who was flying it. He is in Berlin now. The Perkun
ishans have tried to keep both the machines and their captiv
secret, but we have our ways of getting information."

Two Hawks swore. He had been so preoccupied with hi
own affairs that he had not once thought of the German plane
that had appeared at the same time the *Hiawatha* had gon
through the gate. Of course! The German aviator must als
have come into this world.

"You are in great danger," Ilmika said. "Just as we know
about this . . . this German . . . so the Perkunishans know
about you. And they believe that you are from another uni
verse. You are a threat to them because you have knowledge o
weapons and machines superior to those of Eorthe. Undoubt
edly, the Perkunishans plan to use the German's knowledge
and skill. But they don't want yours to be used by their
enemies. So . . ."

"So they'll try to kill us the first chance they get," Two
Hawks said. "I'm surprised they haven't already tried."

"Maybe they've hesitated because, if they failed, it would
convince the Hotinohsonih government that your story is
not a madman's. But now that the city will soon be under

siege, they might try under cover of the confusion. They could try tonight. Or even now, during the bombing."

"In that case, you could be in danger, too," he said. "Your government must think me very valuable if it's willing to risk your life in an effort to get me on its side."

She waved a hand and said, "There are guards stationed around the house while I'm here. We'd like to leave them to protect you and O'Brien, but the Hotinohsonih might wonder why."

Two Hawks looked up through the window at the dirigibles. He thought that if the Perkunishans wanted to kill them, they could have ordered the asylum bombed. Yet the big airships were coming nowhere near the building. It was possible that the enemy would prefer taking them alive under the old proverb that two birds, in this case three, in the hand were better than one in the bush, or underground.

This might be true. However, he was sure that the Perkunishans would have no compunctions in killing the two otherworlders if they saw they could not be taken alive.

It was also probable that the Blodlandish were thinking along the same lines. Rather than allow the Perkunishans to capture the aliens and use their knowledge, the Blodlandish would kill the two.

Nobody loves us, Two Hawks thought. He laughed then. It was two against a hostile world. So be it. Whatever happened to him and O'Brien, the others would have to pay a price.

Two Hawks, grinning, turned away from the window to face the Lady Thorrsstein. He said, "So why doesn't your government tell the Hotinohsonih what they know? The Hotinohsonih could throw up a guard around the asylum or else hustle us off to a safe place."

He was surprised to see her blush. Evidently, she was not a professional agent. She had some sense of honor and was only being used because she had a legitimate reason to visit him.

"I don't know," she said. She hesitated, then blurted, "Yes, I do! I was told that the Hotinohsonih wouldn't let you go. They'd keep you for themselves, and that'd be stupid! They don't have time to develop anything you might give them. They'll be too busy fighting for their land, which they're going to lose in any case. Telling them about you would be throwing you away.

"You must get to Blodland. We have the brains and the materials and the engineers and the time to use them. The Hotinohsonih can't hold out for long."

"I don't know about that," he said. "They have lots of country to go yet. Losing 'Estokwa doesn't mean they're licked."

He thought of the great sectors of territory gobbled up by the Germans in Russia, the staggering loses of men and material suffered by the Russians. Yet, they were not only still fighting; they were driving the German back. Of course, the Russians could not have done this without American supplies, and this world had no America.

"All right," he said. "I'll go to England."

"Where?"

"Pardon me. Blodland. The question is, how do we get there?"

"You be ready," she said. "Tonight at midnight."

"You can't get me out of here without force," he said. "Are your men going to shoot their way in? Maybe kill citizens of your allies? Couldn't that create a serious diplomatic situation? And if it's unsuccessful, wouldn't the Hotinohsonih catch on to the fact that they might have something very valuable in their possession?"

"Never mind that. We know what might happen."

She rose to her feet. "This man O'Brien. Is he well enough to get out under his own power?"

"He isn't up to running very far or very fast," Two Hawks said. He frowned. It was obvious that the Blodlandish would not leave O'Brien behind to be used by the Hotinohsonih or Perkunishans. Not alive anyway.

"If you kill him," he said, "the deal's off. You'll have to kill me, too."

She looked shocked. He wondered if she were acting or if she really had not considered such a possibility.

"I . . . I'm sure my people wouldn't do such a thing. You don't know us. We're not savages. We are Blodlandish."

He grinned and said, "Secret agents are alike—German, Yankee, Russian, Perkunishan, Hotinohsonih, Blodlandish, you name them. National security is at stake, and murder means nothing to preserve it.

"All right. Come for us. But you damn well be sure to tell your people that I don't go unless O'Brien goes."

"Don't you dare talk to me like that!" she cried. Her face was red, and her eyes were narrowed. "You . . . you . . ."

"Commoner. Savage," he said. "Where I come from, we don't have royalty or nobility or any such parasitical and oppressive classes. It's true we have our parasites and oppressors, but they're not usually born to that condition. They achieve it through hard work or connivery. Everybody is born equal—in theory, anyway. The practice isn't perfect, but it's better than none.

"And don't forget I'm from a world more advanced than yours. There you'd be the barbarian, the ignorant and not-too-clean savage, not me. And the fact that here you're a direct descendant of the great Dane Thorrsstein Blothaxe and of King Hrothgar doesn't mean an ox-turd to me. I'd tell you to put that in your pipe and smoke it, except it wouldn't mean anything to you."

Her face twisted and turned red; she spun on her high heels so violently that she almost fell. He was still chuckling after the door slammed behind her. A moment later, he did not think things so funny. O'Brien could not go far before needing a rest. Then what?

He returned to his room. The sergeant was in bed, on his back and one arm over his face. Hearing Two Hawks enter, he lifted his arm and turned his head. "One of the attendants told me you had a visitor. The Ilmika broad. How come you late?"

In a low voice, Two Hawks described his conversation. O'Brien whistled and said, "I sure hope they got a car. I just ain't up to much exertion. And how the hell they going to get us out of the country?"

"Probably through the Black Sea and the Dardanelles. The Perkunishan fleet is operating in the Iginth, but a small boat could get through them. After that, I don't know."

"I'm going to need all the strength I can get. Tell you what. The food isn't bad here, though it tastes kind of funny, the way they cook it. But I been hungry for a big thick bowl of potato soup. My mother used to make it for me all the time. Hot, thick, creamy, with onions. Mmmmm. Do you suppose you could talk the cook into putting it on the menu?"

Two Hawks sighed and looked sad. O'Brien's look of expectancy and rapture died. He groaned and said, "Oh no. Co on now. Don't tell me the good old Irish potato . . ."

Two Hawks nodded. "It originated in the Andes of South America."

O'Brien cursed. "What a hell of a world! No tobacco. No turkey for Thanksgiving. And, oh, God, no potatoes!"

Two Hawks said, "Well, you can be thankful for one thing. There's no syphilis. But, knowing your recklessness and horniness, you better watch out for gonorrhea."

"In my condition, that's the least of my worries."

O'Brien closed his eyes and in a minute was snoring. Two Hawks wanted to discuss a plan for that night, but he decided it could wait. O'Brien needed all the sleep he could get. Besides, what could the two of them do but roll the dice and see how they came up?

8

MIDNIGHT ARRIVED with agonizing slowness. It was silent in the asylum except for a rumble of thunder from west and north. The room had only a small window placed two feet above his head. The door was thick oak, ribbed with iron, and locked on the outside. Although Doctor Tarhe gave his better patients plenty of freedom during the day, he made sure they were secure at night.

Faintly, the clang of the big clock down the hall came through the door. Two Hawks counted the strokes. Twenty-four. Midnight.

A panel in the door opened and made him start. Through half-closed eyes, he could see the light of a kerosene lamp shining through the narrow panel. He could also make out the broad-faced, big-nosed visage of Kaisehta', an attendant, making his rounds. The panel closed; Two Hawks got out of bed. He shook O'Brien, who sat up, saying, "You didn't think I'd be sleeping at a time like this?"

Both were already fully dressed. They had nothing to do now but wait for developments. Two Hawks wished he had his weapons, the derringer and the automatic. Tarhe had told him that the secret police had kept the guns for a while, studying them, then had given them to Tarhe. The doctor kept them locked up in a big wall-safe in his study. At the time he was told about them, Two Hawks had wondered why the police did not consider the automatic as an evidence of the truth of his story. Nothing like it existed in this world. But the guns had been returned without comment to Tarhe, and Two Hawks could only deduce that the police considered the automatic to be one more testimonial to his madness. If so, they must be a singularly unimaginative group.

The two sat in silence on the edge of their beds. They did not have long to wait. There was a yell from down the hall. It was chopped off, and a moment later a clinking sound told them a key was being turned in the big padlock. A bolt shot back; the door swung open. Two Hawks stood up, not knowing whether he should expect rescue or death from a gun. Six men wearing hoods stood in the corridor. Their clothes were lower-class Hotinohsonih civilian wear. Two held six-shooters; two, single-shot rifles; two, long knives.

A thickset man spoke Hotinohsonih in a deep bass. He spoke it with a foreign accent. "Are you Two Hawks and O'Brien?"

Two Hawks nodded and said, "Give us guns. Or knives, anyway."

"You have no need of them."

"I have two of my guns locked in the wall-safe," Two Hawks said. "One of them is an automatic pistol, a rapid-fire mechanism that would greatly improve the fire power of the Blodlandish. I need it for a model."

The thickset man hesitated, then said, "It'd take too long to get it from the safe. We don't have the time to drill and blow."

"I know the combination," Two Hawks said. "I've stood behind Doctor Tarhe and watched him enough. He's rather absent-minded."

"Very well. But hurry. We don't have much time."

Two men preceded the others down the hall. Deep Voice gestured with his pistol for the two Americans to go before him. At the end of the hall, the attendant who had cried out, Kaisehta', lay face up on the floor. The top of his head was bloody; his eyes and mouth were open. The skin beneath the dark pigment was a bluish-grey.

"The sons of bitches didn't have to kill him!" O'Brien said. "Poor fellow! I didn't understand a word he ever said to me, but he could make me laugh. He was a good Joe."

"No talking," Deep Voice said. They went down another hall, across the dining-room and into Tarhe's study. Two Hawks pulled up the painting that was supposed to hide the safe. By the light of a flashlight held by Deep Voice, he turned the dial, marked with the numbers of the modified Akhaivian alphabet. The door swung open, and he found his derringer and automatic in a small cardboard box.

Deep Voice extended his hand for the weapons. Reluctantly, Two Hawks gave them to him. Evidently, they were as much prisoners of the Blodlandish as of their former captors.

The party left the studio and went to the main front

door of the asylum. Two men with rifles stepped out on the big verandah and a minute later came back with an all-clear. Two Hawks and O'Brien, followed by the other four Blodlandish, stepped through the door. The city down below was dark except for fires here and there that had not yet been put out. The moon was behind thick dark clouds.

They started down the steps, their destination two autos. These were parked behind shrubbery along the curve of the driveway to their left. The front ends of the cars were barely visible. Just as the two riflemen reached the ground, the flash and bang of guns came out of the shrubbery. Two Hawks pushed O'Brien hard towards the ground and then hurled himself down the steps and out in a dive.

He hit the bare dirt with a force that almost knocked the breath from him and rolled sideways. When he was in the shrubbery that grew along the base of the verandah, he stopped. More fire spurted from the small arms of the men in the bushes. The two Blodlandish who had been in front of him were on the ground at the foot of the steps. One was wounded or dead. The other fired at the Perkunishans from a prone position. Two Hawks presumed that the attackers were Perkunishans and they had come with the same idea as the Blodlandish but a little later.

A man above Two Hawks screamed. A body fell over the verandah railing just above him and crashed down on his legs. By then the other Blodlandish had scattered for cover behind posts and the railing of the verandah. A Perkunishan toppled from the bushes. The others took up a new position behind the Blodlandish cars. Lights were coming on in the house and outlining the men on the verandah. A Blodlandish slumped over the railing, his gun falling into the ground under the bushes near Two Hawks. The man with the rifle grunted and quit firing.

Two Hawks crawled to the gun that the agent had dropped. With this in his hand, he left the relative safety of the steps and bushes and snaked towards the dead or unconscious rifleman. Using the body as cover, he searched through its pockets. He found several small boxes, slid one open, and felt cylindrical shapes packed within. They were linen cartridges with brass percussion caps.

He examined the revolver with his fingers, broke it open, and filled the six chambers. Behind him, O'Brien groaned and said, "I'm hit. My arm's numb. Oh, Christ, I'm bleeding! I'm going to die!"

"Shut up about dying," Two Hawks said. "You sound too strong to be badly hurt."

He rolled over and felt O'Brien's upper left arm. His fingers came away sticky. O'Brien said, "I'm going fast. The life's pumping out of me with every beat of my heart."

"Quit crying," Two Hawks said. "You just think you're dying, maybe because you want to. It's only a flesh wound and not very deep at that."

"You ain't the one who's hit."

Two Hawks raised his head to look over the body. Two men on the verandah and two behind the cars were still shooting. Then one—he looked like Deep Voice—turned to shoot through the window behind him at the light bulbs outlining him. There was a sound as of a fist hitting flesh, and he flew forward. He pitched on his face and was lost from Two Hawks' view except for one foot. His revolver, however, launched from a nerveless hand, broke the window.

The survivor ran for the corner of the house. He bent over while he ran and fired at the Perkunishans. Their bullets smacked into the wooden walls. Just as he reached the corner, he sprawled out and slammed into the floor. Two Hawks supposed that, since he did not get up, he was either hit or playing possum. If he was acting, he had done a good job, since his gun had also clattered on the floor.

"Two Perkunishans left—that I know of," Two Hawks whispered to O'Brien. "And they must have orders to take us dead or alive. Maybe they don't care which, otherwise they'd not have cut loose at us in the dark."

He looked over the body again. He could see no men. They were probably crouching behind the cars, reloading their revolvers and discussing a plan of attack. They could not safely presume that everybody was dead or incapacitated. They would have to come out from behind the cars.

Nor would they have much time to check. There was much noise in the house, voices shouting questions, a patient screaming, and the sound of feet running back and forth. They would have tried to phone the police, but the wires would have been cut.

Nevertheless, the gunfire could attract the police patrols on the streets in the city below. They could soon be coming up the winding hill, and, if they did, the Perkunishans would

find their car blocked. Unless, that is, they had left their vehicle below and had come up on foot.

Two Hawks waited patiently, his revolver cocked. O'Brien
groaned, and Two Hawks told him to shut up. He removed the
long knife from the scabbard of the fallen rifleman. With one
hand, he hefted it and tested its balance. It would make a
good throwing knife and would give him a fair chance to
demonstrate how effective his hundreds of hours of practice
had been.

The Perkunishans had decided to proceed cautiously. One
ran out from behind the car and towards the protection of the
corner of the verandah. Two Hawks let him go. It was too
difficult in the dark and at this distance to make sure of a
hit with the revolver. Besides, if he refrained from firing, he
might convince them they had nothing to fear.

Slowly, he rolled over away from the body and swiveled
around to face the shrubbery at the other curve of the drive.
As he had suspected, the second agent had gone through the
bushes to approach the other end of the verandah. Two Hawks
heard a twig cracking during a brief cessation of noise from
the house. He crawled back to O'Brien and into the bushes at
the base of the verandah. His back was soaked with the sweat
of fear, and his skin felt as if it were bristling.

When he reached the point where the verandah abruptly
curved to go along the side of the house, he stopped. He
waited and then, as he had hoped, the Perkunishan dashed
from the bushes toward the shrubbery behind which he
crouched. Two Hawks shifted the knife to his right hand and
the gun to his left. He arose, and, just as the man crashed into
the bush, Two Hawks thrust the point of the knife into his
throat.

The agent burbled and fell to his knees. Two Hawks pulled
the knife out, stepping to one side to avoid the spurt of blood
The man fell over on his side.

The other Perkunishan called out. Two Hawks spoke softly
in the only Perkunishan phrases he knew, deliberately making them indistinct. Satisfied with this, the other agent left the
corner of the verandah. Two Hawks stepped out from the
bushes and walked confidently towards him. In the darkness,
the Perkunishan would not be able to recognize his silhouette
until he got close, or so Two Hawks hoped. The agent, however, must have been able to see well enough by the light
from the windows of the house. He shouted and fired. His

shout gave Two Hawks enough warning to throw himself to
one side and into the bushes. The bullet screamed by. There
was the sound of shoes on the crushed stone. Two Hawks,
looking out, saw him disappear around the car. He leaped up,
heedless of noise, and ran across the driveway into the tall
shrubbery. When he was several yards from the vehicle, he
slowed down and walked silently.

A dim bulk was moving soundlessly except for the crunch-
ing of wooden wheels on the broken stones. For a minute,
Two Hawks thought that the car was being pushed. Then the
absurdity of such an act became apparent, and he knew the
car was steam-operated. He ran forward. Again, he traded
weapons with his hands, placing the knife in his right. Why
waste a bullet he might need later? Besides, if he should miss,
the Perkunishan would have no lance of flame from a gun
muzzle to show him where his enemy was.

He burst out of the shrubbery just alongside the car. The
driver sat on the right side, since traffic went on the left lane
in this country. But the left window was down and so offered
no obstacle. The knife struck true, going through the open
window and into the side of the neck of the driver. The driver
slumped forward. Two Hawks ran around in front of the car,
which continued its slow backing up.

He jerked the door open, reached in, and pulled the
corpse out by its arm. He did not have time to retrieve his
knife. Once in the driver's seat, he frantically tried to locate
the proper controls. Fortunately, he had seen illustrations of
operating apparatus of steamers in Tarhe's library and had
studied them for just such an occasion.

Two short sticks on a horizontal table projecting from the
instrument panel regulated direction and speed. The left one
moved right or left to steer. The right one, when pushed forward, resulted in forward acceleration. Before discovering
this, Two Hawks had stopped the car with the foot pedal on
the floor, although it protested at the strain between brakes
and engine. Two Hawks placed the speed stick in neutral,
pushed it forward, learned that the car went forward, and
then pulled the stick towards him. The vehicle went backward.

He drove the car forward and around the curve. With an
almost inaudible chuff of steam escaping and wheels crunch-
ing on the stones, the car moved up to where O'Brien lay. Two
Hawks stopped it and then tried to determine which knobs on
the panel controlled the lights. The first one he turned operated

the single windshield wiper, placed in the center of the shield. To do its job, it had to describe an 180-degree arc. Two Hawks thought that Hotinohsinih cars had a long way to go before they could compete with those of his Earth.

But he was happy that he had at least this much.

He turned another knob. A small panel light and the two front head lights, set on top of the fenders, came on. These were not very powerful, but they were good enough for his purposes. The beams lit up the front of the asylum, the bodies on the verandah and the bodies on the steps and on the driveway. He yelled at O'Brien, who rose slowly and walked to the car.

"You're doing all right, lieutenant," he said in a low voice. "But where do we go from here?"

Two Hawks did not answer. He was studying the indicators on the panel. These were glass cylinders set in the middle of the instrument panel. There were six, illuminated by lights behind them. Each had a lighted symbol above it, the symbols being derived from the ideographic writing the Hotinohsonih had used before abandoning it for the Greek alphabet. At various levels, a pale red fluid was rising in each tube, across which were white gradations. The tubes apparently indicated the level of water supply, temperature of steam, amount of fuel, the speed, the battery condition, and the mileage. Two Hawks knew what the degree marks were supposed to mean, but since the Hotinohsonih had a peculiar measuring system, he had trouble converting them into English units.

The water and fuel indicators showed full. As for the speed, he would judge by the seat of his pants. He waited until O'Brien got into the seat beside him, then started down the steep and winding road that led to the city below. Behind them, men emboldened by the absence of gunfire, burst out of the house. At that moment, the moon broke clear of the clouds. He turned off his lights and drove more swiftly by the illumination of the moon. On reaching the bottom of the hill, he stopped the car and got out to look at a street sign. The fact that there was one there showed that he was near a main highway, since very few streets had signs. In the residential districts, a stranger either had to have a map or ask questions if he wanted to find his way around.

His study of the map of 'Estokwa in the library had familiarized him with the main arteries of exit. He was only a few blocks from the great highway which led east. Actually, he had known this, but he wanted to confirm the accuracy of the map.

They rounded a corner and there, at the end of the street, was the highway. Now they could hear the noise of traffic, the murmur of voices, and the creak of axles. The highway was jammed with refugees, men, women, and children carrying big bundles or pushing wheelbarrows or drawing two-wheeled carts loaded with all they could take.

The appearance of confusion was misleading. After Two Hawks had edged the car between two groups, he found that soldiers, stationed every few blocks, were directing traffic. These carried kerosene lamps or large flashlights. The first trooper did not stop their car, but Two Hawks wondered how far they would get before being asked for identity papers. Without these, they could be arrested, perhaps even shot on the spot. So, at the first chance, he swung the car back onto a sidestreet.

"We'll have to take a chance, hope we don't get lost," he said. "And when we're forced back onto the big highway, we may have to make a break for it, ram through a guard post."

"That's all right," O'Brien said, "but where are we going?"

"How's your arm?" Two Hawks said.

O'Brien groaned and said, "I'm bleeding to death. I ain't going to make it, lieutenant."

"I don't think it's that bad," Two Hawks said. He stopped the car and examined the wound in the brightness of a flashlight he had found in a box under the panel. As he had thought, the wound was shallow. There was still a little flow of blood, which was, however, easily stanched with a handkerchief. He bound it around the arm and resumed driving.

O'Brien's reactions had puzzled him until recently. The sergeant had been a good soldier, very competent, cheerful, and courageous. But ever since he had realized that they were out of their native universe, he had changed. He felt as if he were going to die. And this, Two Hawks thought, came from a sense of utter dislocation. He was cut off forever from the world in which he had been born and lived. He was an alien in a place he did not understand. He was suffering from a homesickness the like of which no man had ever experienced. It was literally killing him.

Two Hawks knew how he felt, although he was sure he did not suffer to the same degree. In the first place, he had learned to live with a similar feeling on his native Earth. A child of two cultures, never wholly in phase with either and not believing fully in the values and mores of either, he, too, had been a stranger. In the second place, he was basically more flexible than O'Brien. He could survive the shock of transplantation, rally, and even thrive if things went right. But he was worried about O'Brien.

9

TWO HOURS LATER, after being lost a dozen times, they came out on the main highway, the *kadziiwa'* road. A half-mile away was a large number of soldiers. Even as Two Hawks watched them, they took a man from a car and marched him off to a tent at one side of the road.

"Checking for spies and deserters," Two Hawks said. "All right; we'll go around them."

That was not so easy. They had to cut across a shallow creek a mile away. They drove through slowly without getting stuck only to be stopped five minutes later by a stone fence which seemed to run to both horizons. By then, dawn had come. The car paralleled the fence for a mile and a half, which finally ran out. However, a dense grove of trees and a broad creek further barred them.

Two Hawks drove the vehicle into the stream, which was about thirty yards wide. They plowed ahead for ten yards with the water beginning to seep from under the doors. Then the car stopped, its wheels spinning. Nothing after that could get it out of the mud.

"We'll hoof it," Two Hawks said. "Maybe it's just as well the car got stuck. If we'd gone on, and the water got too deep, the boiler might've blown up."

"Now you tell me! Let's get to hell out of here!"

They traveled over the farm country paralleling the high way. Four days later, the paved portion ran out. From there on, the road was dirt.

The two ate from food stolen from the peasants. Two days passed. They had a chance to steal a car, an internal-combustion type, and they took it. They made thirty miles that day, cutting along the side of the road, blowing their horn at the refugees in their path. Then, hearing of a check station ahead, they turned onto a narrow dirt rural road. When they had run out of gas, they continued on foot.

"The nation of Itskapintik is to the north," he told O'Brien. "The last I heard, it was neutral. We'll cross the border and throw ourselves on whatever mercy they have."

"I don't like the way you said that," O'Brien said. "What kind of people are they?"

"Basically, Indians with a lot of white genes. They speak a language belonging to the Nahuatl family, something like the Aztec speech of Mexico. They're much like the Aztecs, in fact. They came out of Asia about the same time as the Iroquois, both pushed out by a powerful Amerind nation that later conquered half of northern Asia.

"The Iskapintik defeated another tribe, half-white, half-Amerind, that had just finished terrorizing eastern Europe. The Iskapintik slaughtered half of them and enslaved the rest."

"They're pretty rough, huh?"

"I got that impression. For instance, it was only fifty years ago that they quit sacrificing people at religious ceremonies. And their slaves are not only treated as sub-humans but have no chance of becoming freemen, as they do among the Hotinohsonih."

"Then why are we going there?"

"Not really with the idea of throwing ourselves on their mercy. We'll try to cut across the country, hide from them, travel at night. Our goal will be Tyrsland, Earth 1's Sweden. Perkunisha has declared war against Tyrsland, but it's not made any belligerent moves against it. If we could get there, we could arrange to be transported to Blodland. We'd be important men there; we'd really have something to live for."

"Sweet Mother of Christ! I'd give my right eye to live in a place where they speak English."

"I don't want to discourage you," Two Hawks said. "But you'd have to learn it all over again. However, it would be easier for you than Iroquoian."

They had been cutting across the back-country, using rural roads as guides but keeping parallel with them. Only at night, when the roads were deserted, did they take to them. Even then, Two Hawks did so reluctantly. But walking on fields of wheat or meadows or through the woods slowed them down so much that they had to chance the swifter means of travel now and then. Fifteen days after leaving 'Estokwa, they came across a main highway, going north. From the hilltop, he could see that the great river of refugees had not diminished.

At this point there were no soldiers evident, so he decided that it would be safe to mingle with the traffic.

For two days they trudged along on the fringe of the column, finding that they could make better time this way. The dawn of the third day, they heard cannonfire to the west. By nightfall, the rattle of small firearms came from a distance. The next day, Hotinohsonih troops appeared. They were reinforcements from the south, headed for the northwest where a battle raged. Two Hawks and O'Brien went back into the middle of the refugee column to make themselves inconspicuous. Besides, the reckless speed of the military vehicles on the side of the road made travel there dangerous.

The fourth day, at noon, the refugees were diverted eastward at a crossroads. Two Hawks said, "The Perkunishans must have taken the road up ahead. They're really advancing."

"I always thought the Iroquois was mighty warriors," O'Brien said. "But they don't seem to be doing any better than the Russians."

Two Hawks was a little irritated, as if criticism of the Hotinohsonih was, in a way, a criticism of him. He knew that O'Brien always thought of him as an Indian and that, although never outwardly disrespectful, he had his private opinions.

"I'll tell you one thing," Two Hawks said. "The Perkunishans may be winning, but they're paying a hell of a higher price for it than the Germans did. War's a little different here. There aren't any Geneva Conventions, you know. What a nation does with its prisoners of war is strictly its own business. The Perkunishans have found out from previous experience that the Iroquois don't make good slaves. They either keep on trying to escape or get killed trying.

"So Perkunisha has declared a no-quarters war. No prisoners except when one is needed for information. And they torture to get that information. The Hotinohsonih know this; they fight to the death. And when they retreat, they kill their own wounded if they aren't able to carry them out. As a result, the invaders are getting a much stiffer resistance than they otherwise would. But their superior technology and their strategy of bypassing pockets of defenders behind to be mopped up later accounts for their present speed. Plus the fact they're willing to suffer high casualties.

"You see, Perkunisha wants to conquer as much territory as possible before winter comes. This land occupies the same area as southern Russia of Earth 1, without the relatively mild climate. Because of the weak Gulf Current, Europe is subarctic cold in winter. That's another reason why we have to get to Tyrsland before the snows come. We don't want to get caught in the open country then; we'd freeze to death in short order."

O'Brien shivered and said, "Brother, what a world! If we had to go through a "gate," why couldn't we have been lucky and found a nice warm and peaceful world?"

Two Hawks smiled and shrugged. There might be such a "parallel" Earth, but if so, they were not in it. They had to live in the one luck had dealt them.

A few minutes later, they passed a car stuck in the soft earth on the side of the road. Three men were trying to push it out. Two Hawks said, "Did you notice the woman at the wheel? She had a scarf around her hair, and the face was pretty dirty. But I'll swear it was Ilmika Thorrsstein."

He hesitated for several minutes, then decided that her presence might be a lucky break. Maybe she was heading for Itskapintik because her position as daughter of the Blodland ambassador would ensure her good treatment and even a return to her country. She would want to take Two Hawks and O'Brien with her. After all, that had been her original intent, and he could think of no reason why she should have changed her mind.

He walked boldly up to her. For a minute, she seemed puzzled. Then she recognized him. Incredulity was succeeded by a smile of joy. "Can we go with you?" he said.

She nodded and said, "This seems too good to be true."

He did not waste any more time. The two Americans went to the rear of the car and helped the other three men. After the vehicle had regained the harder dirt, Two Hawks and O'Brien got into the front seat beside Ilmika. The others, who turned out to be members of the British embassy at 'Estokwa, rode in the rear. Ilmika drove the steamer as fast as she could without endangering the pedestrians. She used her horn frequently to warn them out of the way, and if they did not dodge quickly enough, swung onto the shoulder. It was just such a maneuver that had trapped her in the mud ten minutes before Two Hawks came along.

While they rode, he told Ilmika what had happened. She knew, of course, that the Blodland agents had been killed, but she had supposed that the Perkunishans had succeeded in abducting the two otherworlders. She was now on this road because her original avenue of escape had been cut off. The Perkunishan fleet had broken into the Black Sea, defeated the Hotinohsonih navy and the small contingent of Blodland ships. They controlled the waters and the air of the Black Sea. The small dirigible on which she had planned to take the two to Pahlavia (Turkey) had been destroyed. So she had fled towards Itskapintik.

They drove all day and night, and dawn found them much further northward but also out of fuel. They had no luck trying to get more from the army vehicles that passed them. Of the twenty, not one stopped in response to their signals.

"It's a long way, but we'll have to walk," Ilmika said. "If I can get into contact with an officer, I might be able to get another car."

She did not sound hopeful. It was evident that the Hotinohsonih were too occupied with the battle to the northwest to spare time or material, even for the Lady Ilmika Thorrsstein. And they had walked no more than four miles, when they got evidence that the soldiers were too busy taking care of themselves to bother with them.

A score of troopers a half-mile ahead ran from a woods and cut across the road. The refugees near them abandoned their carts and ran after them. Word passed back along the column and with it panic. The road suddenly became a litter of vehicles and no people.

Forty yards ahead of them, the earth blossomed into a pillar of upflung dirt and smoke. The people who had just deserted the highway were unhurt, but the next shell exploded near a group who had not heard the news in time. They were tossed in every direction.

Two Hawks and the other had flung themselves in a small ditch when the first shell landed. They hugged the earth while a second, third, and fourth, running down the road, deafened them and covered them with dirt. A severed foot landed by Two Hawks' head. He took one look and then drove his face into the grass. The fifth shell stunned and half-buried them, but no one was hit. The sixth exploded a little further down; the seventh struck the ditch and killed a number of men, women, and children.

Then the cannonade ceased. Two Hawks raised his head. Across the road was a burnt-out wheat field and beyond it a sloping hill. Over the top of the hill came five armored cars. Two carried long-snouted cannons; the others were armed with weapons that looked from this distance like the barrels of machine guns. Two Hawks knew that machine guns had not been invented yet. In fact, this was one of the items he had intended to explain to the Blodlandish. But he did not like their looks, although the cannons would have been enough for him to decide on flight. He rose with the others and dashed across the blackened stubble of the wheat field on his side of the road. He had seen the Iroquois troops take cover in a copse of trees about a quarter-mile to the northwest. They would be the object of attack by the armored cars, so there was no use trying to hide there. He led the others southeast across the field towards a distant line of half-burned trees that probably hid a stream. By the time the refugees had reached the middle of the field, the Perkunishans had crossed the road. They fired a few rounds at the group, which kept on running. Glancing behind him, Two Hawks could see the bullets throw up fragments of earth. The rate of fire amazed him. He was sure that the cars had some sort of rapid-fire weapon. His reading had not indicated the existence of such a gun, but it was evident that it must have been developed secretly and only now revealed.

One more reason for the Perkunishans' rapid advances. Their firepower must be overwhelming.

The cars swung towards the woods, and soon the racket of battle was hideous. It lasted for perhaps ten minutes. After that, a silence. By then the refugees had passed through the tree-lined creek and had entered a relatively thick and extensive woods. They walked until nightfall, slept several hours, then resumed their flight. Two days afterwards, they came upon a group of dead soldiers. A gully near them concealed a small car—equivalent of a jeep—which was undamaged and had a half-tank of gas. They drove it northward until the fuel ran out and began walking again. A week later, they were somewhere near the Itskapintik border.

They had heard light rifle fire ahead of them. While Ilmika and a man who had been sick hid behind some trees, the others crawled up the slope of a hill. They were armed with rifles and revolvers taken from the dead who had also provided them with the jeep. Nevertheless, they did not intend to take any aggressive action. They just wanted to determine what the situation ahead was and if they would have to take a wide detour.

He got to the top of the hill and inspected the fight through binoculars. The skirmish was almost at an end. There were a number of bodies on the ground at various distances outside a stone rampart, all that was left of a farmhouse which had burned. The bodies wore the black and orange uniforms of the Perkunishan infantry. There were seven attackers left, and they were working in closer to the defense behind the wall. Two Hawks watched for a while and saw that only three were still firing from the wall. Then a Perkunishan, crouching behind an overturned wagon near the ruins, threw a grenade. It landed over the wall and in a corner.

After the explosion, there was no return fire. Still cautious, the Perkunishans continued to hug the ground until they were several yards away. One exposed himself briefly but drew no fire. There was a signal from one, and all rose and dashed towards the wall. Suddenly, smoke from a gun behind the wall rose, and seconds later Two Hawks heard the crack. A Perkunishan fell. Another shot; another crumpled.

The others were too near the wall to turn to run. They kept on charging but fired as they did so to force their enemy to keep his head down. He, however, paid no attention to the bullets which were bouncing off the stone near his head. He kept on shooting and with deadly effectiveness. Two more staggered; one fell backward and the other ran forward again a few steps after stopping before he too slumped.

Two Hawks was surprised. He could see the helmet and upper part of the defender's uniform. Both were the same type as the Perkunishans'. There was one difference. He wore two broad red stripes on his chest.

Then the survivors were through a break in the wall. They fired pointblank at him, but if he was struck he gave no indication. He reversed his rifle, swung the stock like a club, and felled the closest man. He disappeared momentarily from Two Hawks' view, then came up with the body of the man he had struck down held above his head. He hurled the body at the other two and knocked them both down. What he might have done after that, however, was matter for speculation. He seemed to have the upper hand all of a sudden, but one of the men who had been shot down came to life. He rose and fired at the man with the red stripes. The helmet flew off his head, and he dropped.

A minute later, the three survivors had dragged their enemy out onto the ground. The wounded Perkunishan did not help them but busied himself shedding his coat and tearing off his shirtsleeve. He then bandaged his upper right arm. The other two hauled the body of the enemy to a place beneath a maple tree. From somewhere they had gotten a rope, a section of which they used to tie his hands. They removed the man's boots and bound his feet together.

One end of the rope was tied to the man's wrists and the other thrown over a branch. Two men hauled on the rope, and the captive was borne upright until his bare feet were about eight inches from the ground. His position must have been painful, since all the strain of weight was on his arms, tied behind him, and forced back and up. Despite this, the face of the hanging man was expressionless. He spun slowly at the end of the rope and did not even open his mouth to protest when the soldiers piled wood for a fire below his feet.

Two Hawks decided to interfere. He admired the big man's magnificent fight, although this alone would not have been enough to make him attack the soldiers. He was curious about the reasons for the fighting between two groups of Perkunishans.

He told the others in his party what he wanted to do. They agreed to follow him, especially after he said he thought the captive might give them valuable information. They spread out, taking some time to go around the hill and crawl along a depression. Entering the woods from the depression, they cautiously approached the Perkunishans. Ten minutes elapsed before they were crouching behind trees, close enough to hear the conversation. Since this was in Perkunishan, Two Hawks did not understand much of it, but it was obvious they were cursing and taunting the hanging man.

By then, the fire was blazing high enough to lick at his bare feet. He had to be suffering intense agony, yet he said nothing. Two Hawks did not wait any longer for a more advantageous time. He did not want the captive to be crippled. He drew a bead on the stomach of the soldier nearest him; the others also sighted in. Two Hawks lifted one hand, held it, then chopped down. An almost simultaneous crash of gunfire smashed the three Perkunishans backwards. None of them moved again.

Two Hawks rushed out, kicked the burning sticks to one side, and then cut the rope where it was tied to the tree-trunk. Two Blodlandish lowered the hanging man.

Two Hawks removed his knife from his scabbard, but he

did not offer to cut the giant's bonds. He looked too dangerous. He was at least six feet seven high and three across
the shoulders. His arms, chest, and legs were gorilloid in
bulk. His face was broad and highcheekboned; his nose,
aquiline; his hair, straight and black. However, his skin was
not especially dark, and his brown eyes had large green
flecks.

One of the Blodlandish, Aelfred Herot, questioned the man
in Perkunishan. There was some rapid conversation, and
Herot said, "He's a Kinukkinuk."

Two Hawks nodded. Kinukkinuk was the Algonquian
nation which occupied the area of Czechoslovakia of Earth 1.
For over a hundred years, it had been part of Perkunisha.

"He says his name is Kwasind, that is, The Strong One.
He was in a Kinukkinuk regiment under the command of Perkunishan officers. He and other Kinukkinuk decided to desert
and join the Hotinohsonih. But they were tracked down and
cornered in the farmhouse. You saw the rest. I've explained
who we are. He says he would like to throw in with us. He
also speaks Hotinohsonih, since his mother was a slave from
that country. He says she was freed by his father before he
married her, so Kwasind is not the son of a slave. The
Kinukkinuk are very proud, even if they are treated as sub-
human by the Perkunishans."

Without a word, Two Hawks cut the ropes from Kwasind.
The giant rubbed his wrists while he walked around to restore
his circulation. The skin of his feet was very red but not
burned. He sat down on a corpse to put his boots back on.
Two Hawks handed him a rifle and a belt of ammunition and
a knife.

In Hotinohsonih, Kwasind said, "Thank you."

"You can walk all right?"

"I can walk. But if you had been ten seconds later . . ."

Two Hawks sent Herot back to bring up Ilmika and her
guard. The casualties were checked. Three Perkunishans were
still living, seriously wounded. Kwasind and the Blodlandish
put them out of their pain with knives in the solar plexus.
Kwasind took a sword from a dead officer and hacked off the
heads of the Perkunishans. He arranged them in a little
pyramid and then stood back a distance to admire the ar-
rangement.

O'Brien vomited. Two Hawks felt sick.

Herot explained. "By severing the heads of his enemies,

he's keeping their souls from going to Michilimakinak, the Kinukkinuk heaven."

"Very interesting," Two Hawks said. "I hope he doesn't have any more customs which will delay us."

Ilmika and Elhson joined them. Ilmika turned pale on see-ing the heads, but she did not say anything.

Kwasind chanted over the bodies of his fellow countrymen, then opened their jackets and shirts. The left breast of each was tattooed with a swastika in a circle. These Kwasind re-moved by cutting a circle around them and stripping off the skin. He restored the fire that Two Hawks had kicked apart and threw the tattooed skins into the flames.

Herot said, "The tattooed symbols contain the 'souls'. If they're burned, the souls are free to fly up to Michilimakinak. But if they're taken by enemies, they could be dried or pre-served in alcohol. The souls would then never get to Mich-ilimakinak."

Two Hawks waited until Kwasind was finished. If the de-lay had been caused by anything but a religious custom, he would have insisted on leaving at once. In this case, it was important not to offend. To strike at a man's religion was to strike at his basic identity.

10

THE PARTY WALKED northwards across the country all that day and the next. The dawn of the third, they were startled out of their sleep by the roar of many motors. Two Hawks crawled to the edge of the hollow in which they were hidden and looked down the slope of the hill at the road a quarter-mile below. It was crowded with a column of armored cars and trucks pulling cannon on caissons. All the vehicles were painted scarlet with blue bars. The doors bore the image of a black bear, rampant.

"Itskapintik," Ilmika said behind him. "They must finally be invading Hotinohsonih. We've known for some time that Perkunisha was trying to persuade the Itskapintik to join them. They've promised half of Hotinohsonih to them."

Two Hawks watched the stream of men, weapons, supplies, and vehicles roar by. The features of the soldiers under the round steel helmets somewhat resembled those of the Mexican Indians of Earth 1, although the skin was lighter.

All day, the column rode by. The watchers from the hill dozed and took turns guarding. They did not dare to venture out in the light, even in the woods, because there were patrols in the countryside. When dusk came, they resumed their march. The next day, Aelwin Graenfield, the sick Blodlandish, could not get up. Weakly, he urged the others to leave him behind. They would not hear of it. He continued to get worse and by dawn was dead.

They placed his body in a shallow grave scooped out with knives. Herot conducted the services, which consisted of a prayer by the Blodlandish as they circled sunwise around the open grave and dropped a fistful of dirt on the body at the bottom. Two Hawks stood with bowed head but watched the proceedings. The Blodlandish, like all west Europeans, sub-scribed to the same religion. This had been founded only a thousand years ago by a man named Hemilka. Inspired by a revelation, he had renounced the worship of the old gods and proposed to replace it with a monotheism. He had been martyred—suspended from a rope by one leg and both legs broken and then left to hang until he died from pain, thirst, and exposure. This was a form of execution for heretics, a form which had died out only seventy-five years ago.

After Hemilka's death, his disciples had scattered to escape the same punishment and also to spread his message. Eventually, Hemilkism triumphed, as the Christianity of Earth 1 had won after a long period of persecution.

There were many parallels to Christianity in Hemilkism: salvation for all who believed in Hemilka, his virgin birth, a heaven, a hell, and a limbo for virtuous pre-Hemilka pagans. There was also a doctrine much like that which the Mormons held, baptism of the dead.

Two Hawks explained the history and tenets of the religion to O'Brien. The sergeant was especially interested and proud that Earth 2's Christ had been an Irishman.

"It's quite a coincidence," Two Hawks said, "that the great western religions of our Earth were founded by Semites. Judaism and Christianity by the Jews and Islam by an Arab who took much of his religion from the previous faiths. But here . . ."

"A mick is God's only son, not a Hebe," O'Brien said. "Didn't you say he was born in Ireland! And who was his mother? Surely, she was Irish, too."

"Curiously enough, she was named Meryam," Two Hawks said.

Graenfield's body was covered with dirt, and they got ready to take up the march. It was then that the Itskapintik police rose from behind the trees where they had been observing the ceremony. There were six, all with single-shot rifles, and ready to fire if the others did not lay down their arms.

The policemen bound the hands of the captives behind them. A small boy, the farmer's son who had reported them to the police, stood proudly to one side.

The chief of the police, a short dark man with a big mouth full of very large protruding teeth, leered at Ilmika. The bound captives could do nothing but stand as passive witnesses to what followed.

Suddenly, O'Brien, who had turned pale and started breathing like a winded horse, gave a whoop and ran forward, escaping the butt of the rifle swung at him. He covered the few

yards between the prisoners and the police before the latter
were aware of what was happening. He leaped into the air,
bent his knees, and then kicked straight out. The policeman,
bending over Ilmika, heard the warning shouts of the others
and turned. His chin took the impact of both of O'Brien's
hard-driven boots. There was a crack as of a stick breaking,
and he flipped onto his back.

O'Brien slammed hard onto his back. His arms, tied behind him, took the brunt of the fall. He cried out with pain
and rolled over and tried to struggle to his feet. A rifle butt
cracked against the back of his head; he pitched forward on
his face. The man who had struck O'Brien reversed his rifle
and shot him in the back of his neck. O'Brien straightened
out, quivered, and was still.

The Itskapintik whom O'Brien had kicked was also dead,
his jaw shattered and neck broken. Furious, the police began
to beat the prisoners. Two Hawks was knocked to the ground
by a rifle butt slammed into his shoulder. He was then kicked
in the ribs twice. Another boot-toe driven into the side of his
head stunned him.

Their fury finally vented, the police quit. They talked
violently among themselves for a while. The prisoners groaned
or moaned or lay mute and motionless. The most brutally
beaten, Herot, vomited through lips torn by a gun butt. Blood
and teeth poured out on the ground.

Two Hawks could not think straight for a while. His head
felt as if a hot spike had been drive into it, and his shoulder
ached like a rotten tooth. Later, he figured out why O'Brien
had acted so suicidally. The sergeant had been slowly dying
ever since he had learned that he was cut off forever from
his native world. A deep grief has possessed him, one so
piercing that his will to live poured out through the skin of
his soul. And so he had deliberately caused his own death. It
was an act of bravery and gallantry and thus did not look
to the others as self-murder. And he had struck back at this
world.

Another blow to him, perhaps the most wounding of all,
had been the knowledge that his religion did not exist here.
He could not attend mass or confess. He would die with no
chance of last unction or of being buried in holy ground.

O'Brien's act was not entirely in vain. It had taken the
interest away from Ilmika. The chief growled an order.

Dazedly, Ilmika struggled to her feet and submitted to having her hands retied.

Herot quit vomiting. He got to his feet and resumed talking to the chief. The Itskapintik told him to shut up, and when Herot continued, the chief placed the muzzle of his revolver against Herot's stomach. The Blodlandish was either out of his mind with grief and pain or else a very brave man who was not going to back down for anybody. From Herot's tone, Two Hawks was sure that a good part of his talking was invective. He expected the chief to blow Herot's guts out. The chief only grinned, shoved Herot away, and ordered the captives aboard a truck which had driven up. They were on the truck ten hours without food or water. The truck finally drove into a military camp. Here the prisoners were marched into a high-walled compound. A little water, some stinking stew and hard dry black bread was given them. Those whose lips and jaws were not too painful from the beatings ate.

Night fell, and with it came a horde of mosquitoes. Morning brought some relief. An officer who could speak both Blodlandish and Hotinohsonih questioned them. Their stories seemed to alarm the officer. Guards came an hour later and took Ilmika away, treating her with courtesy.

Two Hawks asked Herot if he had any idea of what was going on. Herot mumbled through swollen lips and broken teeth, "If Itskiapintik was still neutral, we'd be set free with an apology. But not now. The best we can hope for is a life of slavery. The Lady Thorrsstein will probably be chosen by some high-ranking officer to be his whore. After he's tired of her, she'll go to a lesser officer. God knows what after that. But she's a Blodlandish noble; she'll kill herself at the first chance."

Two Hawks was not so sure. He suspected that something unusual was happening. The following day, he and Kwasind were taken to a building and into an office. Ilmika Thorrsstein, an Itskapintik officer, and a Perkunishan official were also there. The latter was splendid in a scarlet-and-white uniform, many medals, and huge gold epaulets. Ilmika looked much better. She had bathed, her hair was in a Psyche knot, and she was wearing a lady's jacket and long skirt. However, she seemed withdrawn. The Perkunishan had to repeat questions several times before she would respond.

Two Hawks caught on quickly. The very efficient espionage system of Perkunisha had learned about the capture of Ilmika shortly after it had taken place. Its government had immediately "requested" that Ilmika, Two Hawks, and Kwasind be turned over to it. The Itskapintik government may have wondered what was behind the "request," but it had no way of finding out. If it had suspected the truth about Two Hawks, it probably would have denied having him.

It was not until later that Two Hawks found out why Ilmika and Kwasind were also wanted by Perkunisha. Ilmika was a grandniece of its ruler, the Kassandras. She was the daughter of his niece, who had married a younger brother of the king of Blodland. After the king's brother died, the Kassandras' niece had married Lord Thorrsstein, himself a cousin of the king. Ilmika was born of this marriage. The Kassandras did not want his grandniece to fall into the barbarous hands of the Itskapintik.

As for Kwasind, he had been mistaken for O'Brien. That error would soon be detected, but it would last long enough for him to be taken to Berlin with the other two. The Blodlandish were never heard of again. Two Hawks supposed that they were swallowed up in the maw of a labor camp.

Before the three boarded the train that was to take them to Berlin, they witnessed the execution of the chief and his four policemen. These were marched into a courtyard in which were a number of pillars with a projecting horizontal beam on top of each. The police were naked, and their skins were covered with bruises and whipcuts. Their hands were bound behind their backs. The executioners looped the ends of thick wires tightly around one ankle of each of the prisoners. Then they turned cranks which wound the wires around a drum. The prisoners were lifted to a height of six feet by the wires tied around their ankles.

The police were courageous, Two Hawks had to give them credit for that. Two even spat at the executioners. But bravery soon dissolved before the pain of stretching skin. They hung screaming and writhing, the skin lengthening slowly from their weight, until they fainted. Cold water over their naked bodies revived them; they began screaming again. One man fell when his violent contortions caused his ankle to be severed. He was picked up, the wire rewound around his calf, and he was hauled up into the air again.

Two Hawks did not feel sorry for them. They were getting what they deserved. Nevertheless, he felt sick, and he was glad when Ilmika said that she was satisfied that justice was being done. They left the building but had to go a long way before they ceased to hear the screams.

Two Hawks did not think he was going to like what lay ahead of him in Berlin, yet he felt relieved when they crossed the Itskapintik border. Not until then did the uneasiness in his mind go away.

The car in which they rode was, in many ways, luxurious. Two Hawks and Kwasind had a compartment for themselves. The food was excellent, and they could drink as much beer, wine, or whiskey as they wished. They could even take a bath. Nevertheless, there were iron bars over every window, and armed guards stood on both sides of the doors at each end of the car. The officer in charge, a Khiliarkhos (captain) Wilkis, was never far away. He took his meals with the two men and helped Two Hawks with his lessons in Perkunishan.

Ilmika stayed in her compartment. The few times she came out, she seemed constrained. He supposed that it was because he had witnessed her disgrace. Not only did she feel embarrassment that he had seen her suffering an outrage, she probably felt contempt because he had not tried to defend her. In her code, any gentleman would have died rather than permit a noblewoman to be dishonored. Two Hawks did not try to defend himself. She had seen what had happened to O'Brien. Moreover, her own people, Herot and the others, had not fought for her. They had chosen the realistic path—and wisely, he thought. What did she think of them?

Ilmika said nothing about this. She answered Two Hawks' greetings with a cold nod. He shrugged and sometimes smiled. What did he care? He had been attracted to her, but they were abysses apart. He was neither Blodlandish nor noble. Even if she were in love with him—and she had not given the slightest sign she was—she would have to forget about him.

Two Hawks occupied himself in learning the language and also studying the country he saw through the car windows. Its topography, he supposed, would be much like that of Poland and Germany of Earth 1. The dwellings were not too different in structure, although there was a tendency to decorate with what he called "curlicue" architecture. The peasants were dressed simply, were shaggy-haired and not too clean. The absence of horses gave him a strange feeling. There was no plowing at this time, but Wilkis told him that oxen were used, although the beasts were being replaced by steam or gas tractors on the big estates. Wilkis boasted that his country had more farm tractors than any other nation in the world.

At the city of Gervvoge, another officer joined them. Vyautas wore an all-black uniform with silver epaulets and a silver boar's head on his tall red shako. His face was gaunt and thin-lipped, yet he turned out to be affable and quick-witted. He was liable to pun at the slightest or no excuse. Two Hawks was not deceived. Vyautas was there for pre-liminary questioning of the two prisoners.

Two Hawks had decided he might as well tell everything. If he refused to cooperate, he would end up by spilling his guts anyway, and be in very bad health in the bargain. Be-sides, he had no definite loyalties to any country of this world. Fate had originally thrown him in with the Blodland-ish and Hotinohsonih, yet the latter had tortured him and then locked him up and the former had betrayed their own allies to get their hands on him. There did not seem to be much difference between the practices of Perkunisha and Blodland. Yet he did not feel right in becoming an ally of a German. Working for the same nation with which the German flier was working was, in some undefinable way, betraying his own country, his own world.

But—here there was no United States of America, just as there was no Germany.

After a half-hour of interrogation by Vyautas, Two Hawks understood the reasons for the type of questions. Vyautas was checking the answers against those in a large bound volume of typewritten sheets. The book undoubtedly contained in-formation given by the German.

Two Hawks said, "How do you know that the fellow—what-ever his name is—has given you a true story?"

Vyautas was startled. Then he smiled and said, "So you know about him? The Blodlandish told you? His name, by the way, is Horst Raske."

"And what do you think of our tales?"

"There's enough evidence to convince those who matter. To me, though, there are very puzzling aspects. Let's say that there is a universe occupying the same 'space' as ours but not intersecting. I can understand why the same type of animals, including human beings, might develop on both planets. After all, the size and distance of the Earths from the sun are identical, and the geophysical factors are similar.

"But I cannot understand why almost identical languages

are found on both worlds. Do you realize how mathematically improbable such a coincidence is? About several billion billions to one, I would say. Yet, I am asked to believe that not one, but many languages, have their near-counterparts on your Earth."

Vyautas shook his head and said, "No! No! No!"

"Raske and my men passed through a 'gate,'" Two Hawks said. "Perhaps there have been many gates. During the hundred thousand years or so that man has existed, there may have been much traffic between the two Earths. Perhaps mankind did not originate on this planet. He may have come here from my Earth. The fossil evidence in my world indicates that man originated there. However, it's not proven beyond all doubt. No fossils have been found that are undeniably a direct link between modern man and subman."

Vyautas said, "Until fifty years ago, speculation about the evolution of man was forbidden. Even now, there's much resistance to the idea that man may not have been created in one day and that day only 5,000 years ago. However, there is strong evidence that man has existed much more than five millenia. Not only man but several types of subhumans."

"I would maintain that the people of this planet originated on my Earth," Two Hawks said. "Only . . ."

"Only what?"

"If the original men came through gates to this world, then their horses and camels should have come through with them. But say that various tribes of Earthmen did come through in enough numbers to establish themselves here but came at a time *before* the horse and camel were domesticated. That could account for the fact that Earth 2 has any number of ethnic types and languages which are similar enough to certain Terrestrial groups to be descended from them. It might also account for the complete absence of other Earth 1-type peoples here: the Slavs, the Hebrews, the Italics, the Australian aborigine, and so forth.

"Yet, if human beings could come through the 'gates,' why not animals? Why not the horse, the camel?

"Also, it seems peculiar that immigrants from Earth 1, who must have passed over only in small numbers, could have come to dominate regions, the same general regions, as on Earth 1. Why were the people who already occupied those regions, and who must have been more numerous, defeated by the newcomers? I just don't know."

Vyautas said, "I don't know either. But the hard and indissoluble facts are that we Perkunishans and Hellenes and Rasna and so forth are here. And we have to live here, and you are here and also have to live here. So, let's get on with our discussion."

Two Hawks was with Vyautas almost every waking moment of the trip. However, Two Hawks managed to get in some questions of his own. Vyautas did not mind answering, and his manner was such that Two Hawks was convinced his interrogator believed his story. One of the things Two Hawks found interesting was that the concept of zero had originated only three centuries before and had come to Europe only two hundred years ago. As on Earth 1, the concept had come from India to Europe. Moreover it had been transmitted by the Arabs.

Vyautas gave this information, but he was more interested in Two Hawks' disclosure that the Arabia of Earth 1 was rich in oil. Apparently this Arabia was so little explored that oil had not been discovered there. Moreover, the Germans had not told the Perkunishans about it.

"Arabia will have to come under our rule," Vyautas said. "At the moment, the southern coasts are held by Blodland. But we will take their bases away from them. You know, this one item of information makes the whole interrogation worthwhile."

"You would have found out sooner or later from Raske, anyway," Two Hawks said. "What I'd like to know is, what does your government plan on doing with us?"

"Since you are cooperating so well and seem to be a mine of vital information, you'll be treated very well. In fact, we can offer you citizenship. It'll only be a second-class citizenship, of course, because you're not all-white."

Vyautas was silent for a while, then said, "I think it can be arranged to give you a special category. It's been done before. We could make you a first-class citizen by edict of the Kassandras."

11

THE TRAIN PULLED into Berlin late at night, and Two Hawks did not have much opportunity to examine the city. Ilmika, Kwasind, and he were taken in a car which drove swiftly. An armored car preceded it; another followed it. He did get a chance to see the houses and large buildings, all of which had a medieval appearance. The streets were narrow and winding, and the houses abutted directly on the streets. There were gas streetlights but only on the corners of crossroads. Occasionally, a civilian rode by on a bicycle. The riding must have been bumpy because of the lack of rubber tires.

Then they were in the heart of the city. Here, the old buildings had been torn down to make way for wide paved streets and huge buildings with immense pillars in front. They passed a square in the center of which was a stone monument depicting the conquests of the great-grandfather of the present Kassandras or Emperor. A half-mile beyond it was the Palace of the Kassandras himself.

The car stopped in front of the Palace. Ilmika was conducted from the car to the Palace. Before leaving, she looked once at Two Hawks from under the shadow of her hood. She was frightened and she was signalling him for help. He could do nothing, however, except to grin at him and to hold up his two fingers in the sign of the V. She could not know what that meant, but she did manage to smile faintly at him. Then she was gone.

Two Hawks and Kwasind were escorted to another building near the Palace. They went through some huge and magnificently decorated rooms, up two flights of stairs, down a thickly carpeted hall, and into a suite of four rooms. This was theirs until further notice. They were told, however, that the windows had bars over them and that six soldiers were stationed outside their doors. Vyautas then said, "It's very late, but Raske wants to talk to you. I will wait here until he has left you."

A few minutes later, a challenge came from the noncom officer of the guard outside the main door. There was a mumble; the door swung open. A tall, very handsome youth entered. He wore the blue-and scarlet uniform of an officer in the Imperial Guard. He removed his shako, covered with polar bear fur, to reveal a blond crewcut. He was smiling, and his eyes, a deep blue, reflected the warmth of his smile. He had very long and dark eyelashes.

Two Hawks could understand some of Vyautas' remarks about the influence this man was having over the daughter of the Kassandras. He was one of the most handsome men Two Hawks had ever seen, yet he had enough masculinity to escape being called pretty.

The officer clicked his heels, bowed slightly, and said in a rich baritone, "Lieutenant Horst Raske at your service." He spoke in an English which had only a trace of German accent.

"Lieutenant Roger Two Hawks." Two Hawks then introduced Kwasind. Raske barely nodded at him; he knew that Kwasind was one of the inferior races and a man who could not help him in any way. He also knew that Kwasind was there only because Two Hawks had argued that he be kept with him. When the Perkunishans had discovered that Kwasind was not O'Brien, they had intended to take him off to a labor battalion. They did not know that he was a Kinukkinuk and a deserter, otherwise they would have shot him within the hour. But Two Hawks had told Vyautas that Kwasind was a Hotinohsinoh who had escaped with him from the asylum. He demanded that Kwasind be left in his care; he needed a servant. Vyautas had consented.

Raske told Kwasind to bring them some beer. He sat down on a huge sofa covered with wolf-skins, started to put his hand inside his jacket, then stopped. He smiled and said, "I still reach for a cigarette. Well, that's one of the things I'll have to learn to get along without. A small price to pay in a world which offers me—us—so much more than our native planet. I tell you, Lieutenant, we have it made. These people will give us anything for our knowledge. Anything!"

He was watching Two Hawks to observe the effect of his words. Two Hawks sat down on a chair facing the sofa and said, "You seem to have done very well, considering the short time you've been here."

Horst Raske laughed and said, "I'm not one to let the grass grow under my feet. I am a superb linguist; I've already mastered this barbarous language, at least enough for my purposes. Of course, I was lucky in being half-Lithuanian; Perkunishan is remarkably close to my mother's tongue, you know. But you don't think that coincidence is a sign of my lucky star?"

He took the glass of beer offered by Kwasind and raised it to Two Hawks. "A toast, my friend! To our success! Two Earthmen in a strange but not necessarily unhospitable world! Long may we live and thrive! Thrive as we never could back there!"

"I'll drink to that," Two Hawks said. "And let me congratulate you on your remarkable adaptability. Most men would be in a state of shock from which they would never entirely recover."

"You seem to be doing all right," Raske said.

"I'm tough. I eat whatever is placed before me. But that doesn't mean I won't be looking for tastier food."

Raske laughed again. "I like you! You're a man after my own heart. I was hoping you would be."

"Why?" Two Hawks said.

"I'll be frank with you. I'm not quite as self-sufficient as I seem. I am a little lonely, only a little, you must understand, but a little lonely for the companionship of somebody from my Earth." He laughed and said, "I would have preferred a woman, of course, but I can't always get what I want. Besides . . ." He raised his glass and winked at Two Hawks over it. "Besides, I have all the female company I want. The best, too. I have managed to gain the interest, more than interest, I might say, of the daughter of the Kassandras. She wields great influence."

"You need me for more than companionship," Two Hawks said. "What other reason is there for this red-carpet treatment?"

"I'm glad you're not stupid. If you were, you wouldn't be of much use to me. Yes, I need you. In fact, you owe your presence here to the fact that I arranged for you to get here. I have a friend who's high in the espionage service; he told me about the two otherworlders who had been put in the insane asylum. I suggested the kidnapping and . . ."

"Were you also the one who suggested we be killed if we couldn't be captured alive?"

Raske was taken by surprise, but he rallied swiftly. Smiling, he said, "Yes, I did. I couldn't have you giving information to the Hotinohsinoh that would put them on a technological level with the Perkunishans—my adopted people—could I? Wouldn't you have done the same if you had been in my shoes?"

"Probably."

"Of course, you would. But you weren't killed. And you owe your escape from a terrible death in an Itskapintik labor camp to me. It was I who insisted that the Perkunishan government demand your release. Of course, the Kassandras was furious when he heard about how his niece had been violated. He was the one who insisted that the policemen be executed."

"And what will happen to her now?" Two Hawks said.

"She'll be offered citizenship. If she takes the oath, she'll be treated well, very well, as befits the Kassandras' niece. If she refuses, and she's likely to do so, being a stubborn Britisher, she'll be imprisoned. But she'll be in a nice prison, probably have private rooms and servants in some castle."

Two Hawks sipped at his beer and looked at the German. German? Raske had already forgotten about the war on his native world. He was interested only in what he could get for himself here and was delighted that he had something valuable to trade. His attitude, Two Hawks had to admit, was realistic. Why continue the war here? Deutschland and America and Russia might as well be on a planet in another galaxy. The oaths of allegiance he and Raske had taken were as nullified as if both had been killed over Ploesti.

This, of course, did not mean that he trusted Raske. The man was an opportunist. Once he found Two Hawks no longer useful, he would get rid of him. But that attitude could work two ways. Raske could be used by Two Hawks.

"I can be of great value to Perkunisha," Raske said, "because I am an aeronautical engineer. I also know something of chemistry and electronics. But I do not know what your academic background is."

Two Hawks said, "My field isn't going to be of much help, I'm afraid. I have a Master's in Indo-European Linguistics. But I did take a number of courses in mathematics and electronics because I knew that linguistics was eventually going to use these as tools in language analysis. I have a first-class radio operator's license, and I know a lot about automobiles. I worked part-time as a mechanic to put myself through school"

"That's not so bad," Raske said. "I need somebody qualified to be my assistant in developing our radio equipment and airplanes. I've been drawing up plans for a fighter plane; it'll be equipped with radio and machine guns. However, it won't be very advanced. It'll be about the same as a late World War I plane. But it will sweep the skies, send every Blodland lyftship flaming to the ground, and it'll be tremendously useful for observation and for strafing ground-troops."

Two Hawks was not surprised that Perkunisha was not building a modern aircraft. After all, they were of materials that derived from an advanced technology. To make superior steel and aluminum (not even known here), to build the factories which could manufacture such metal and machine them, could be done. But it would take a very long time, and the Perkunishan government would not want such a delay. It desired something that could be used in the near future, not after the war was over.

So Raske would have offered them a craft which would seem obsolete and very inefficient to him, but would be daring, even futuristic, to this world.

Raske continued to talk. He was overburdened with work; he was getting very little sleep. His schedule interfered with his other activities, namely, entrenching himself socially and politically and wooing the daughter of the Kassandras. Fortunately, he needed little sleep and had managed to operate effectively. But he could use a man who would take over the burden of overseeing all the little details and making the daily scores of decisions. Yes, Two Hawks would be a great help.

He pointed at the two-headed wolf symbol of silver on his left breast. "I have a military title which is the equivalent of Colonel in the Luftwaffe. I can arrange to make you a Major as soon as we can get you a special citizenship. Normally, that would take weeks, but we'll get it done by tomorrow. Then you become a full-fledged Perkunishan, by grace of the Kassandras. You couldn't do any better. This country is destined to become the ruler of all Europe and probably of Africa and much of Asia, too."

"Just as Deutschland was?" Two Hawks said.

Raske smiled. "I am not a stupid or unrealistic person," he said. "I could see the handwriting on the wall the moment the United States entered the war. But here, you see, there is no America. Moreover, Perkunisha is relatively more powerful than Germany. Its citizens occupy a much larger area to begin with. Its technology and military tactics are superior to all other nations. And with us two, it will soon have an invincible technology. But these is much work to be done, much work. It takes time to build mills to make a better steel and to make aluminum. We might have to take Greenland before we can get our hands on bauxite. And then the bauxite has to be mined and transported here. And synthetic rubber has to be made. And factories have to be built and new tooling machines made, and these cannot be done without blueprints and a big administration. Thousands have to be trained.

"It's a Herculean task. But it can be done, and what do you think the position of the men who make it possible will be? I ask you, but you need not reply. Oh, we're going to be very very important, Roger Two Hawks. You'll be a great man; you could never have dreamed of such power and wealth when you were a young man on the reservation."

"I never lived on a reservation," Two Hawks said.

Raske stood up, walked over, and put his hand on Two Hawks' shoulder. "I did not mean to hurt your feelings. Do not be so touchy. I do not know what offends you and what pleases you. I will find out some day, when we have time. Meanwhile, let's work together as best we can. And let's not forget what the future holds for both of us."

He walked toward the door but stopped before opening it. "You get some sleep, Roger. In the morning, you can take a bath and then be fitted for new clothes. Then, to work. Work, work, work! And if you get tired, think of what all the drudgery will bring you some day. *Auf wiedersehen*!"

"So long!" Two Hawks said. After the door was closed, he rose and went into the bedroom. The bed was a huge four-poster with velvet curtains on which were depicted scenes from events in Perkunishan history. There was one that showed the torture of a Viking king captured during a raid on Perkunishan territory. Two Hawks did not find it conducive to sleep, but it did make him think. He must use caution in whatever plans he made to escape. That is, if he did try to escape. He had to admit that he was tempted by Raske's offer.

THE GATE OF TIME

Well, why not? On Earth 2, one country was as good as another. He owed no one anything. Even those people closest to him, the Hotinohsinoh people he could easily have identified with, had tortured him and then shut him away in an insane asylum.

At that moment, Kwasind stuck his broad dark face into the room. He asked if he could talk with Two Hawks before he slept. Two Hawks gestured at him to sit down on the bed beside him, but the Kinukkinuk remained standing.

"I didn't understand that language you and Raske were using," he said. "Is it permitted that you tell me what it was all about?"

"Don't talk like a humble slave," Two Hawks said. "You have to be my servant if you want to survive, but that doesn't mean we can't talk man to man when we're alone." He had thoroughly searched the room for listening devices and found nothing. He did not think that electronics was advanced enough to make "bugs" anyway. Still, there was the possibility that eavesdroppers could be hidden behind the wall. He said, "Come on, Kwasind, sit close to me and talk in a low voice."

Two Hawks gave him the meat of his talk with the German. Kwasind was silent for a while, his thick black brows lowered in thought. Then he said, "What this man says is true. You could become a great man, although you would always know that you were a stranger and you would see the contempt behind the smiling and the bowing and great houses and beautiful women they would give you. To the Wapiti (whites), you would always be the upstart barbarian. And when the war is over and they no longer need you, then what? It will be easy to find some reason to disgrace you, to strip you of your title and honors, perhaps even make a slave of you, perhaps even kill you."

"You're trying to tell me something," Two Hawks said. "So far, you're telling me nothing I haven't already thought of."

"They plan to make all Europe into one Perkunisha," Kwasind said. "They are evil. They mean to exterminate the Dakota, the Kinukkinuk, the Hotinohsinoh, and their own allies, the Itskapintik. And the white peoples of Europe will be made to speak the language of Perkunisha; their own languages will be forbidden. Someday, only Perkunishan will be known. The flags of others will be burned; their history books, burned. Some day, every white child in Europe will think of himself as a Perkunishan, not an Iberian, a Rasna, a Blodlandish, an Aikhavian."

"So what's new?" Two Hawks said. "Maybe that'll be the best thing. No more national hates, no more wars."

"You sound like one of them."

"I'm not. But their goals sound fine. Only I don't like the means. But what's the alternative? Are the Blodlandish any better; wouldn't the Kinukkinuk wipe out their hereditary enemies, the Itskapintik and the Hotinohsinoh, if they got a chance? Doesn't Blodland want to extend its dominion over the world? Wouldn't Aikhavia like to resurrect the empire it had under Kassandras the Great?"

Kwasind said, "You told me that you thought slavery was wrong. You said that the white man of Europe of your world had abolished slavery as a great evil, and that the whites of this . . . this America . . . had done the same. You said that the black men and the brown of America were still treated as slaves, but that some day they would be accepted as equals. You said . . ."

"You're leading up to something besides a lecture on ethics," Two Hawks said. "You're sounding me out because you're not sure you should tell me something. Right?"

"You see into my liver and read all that is therein."

"Not quite. But I'll bet ten to one that someone's contacted you about an escape. A Blodlandish has talked to you."

Kwasind nodded and said, "I have to trust you. If I don't, there's no escape. They want you, not me. Now, I talked to you about the evils of Perkunisha because I wanted to get your reaction. I wanted to know how you *felt* about them, not what you thought about them. In your liver, do you *feel* that Perkunisha is wrong? You know that its enemies have their faults but you also know they have a right to work out their own destinies. How do you *feel*?"

Two Hawks rose from his chair and walked over to Kwasind. He put his hand on Kwasind's huge shoulder. "I don't really know about Blodland or the other countries. But I feel that Perkunisha has too many similarities to the Germany of my world. Maybe I could learn to stomach the Perkunishans. I don't really think so."

"That is what I hoped to hear you say."

"Two Hawks said, "If I'd said I was sticking with Perkunisha, you would have killed me, wouldn't you? The Blodlandish want me alive, but if they can't get me, they'll try to make sure their enemy won't have me either. Isn't that so?"

"I won't lie," Kwasind said. "You are my friend; you saved my life. Yet, for my country, I would have killed you with these hands. Then I would have killed as many Perkunishans as I could before they killed me!"

"O.K. So, what's the plan?"

"I'll be told when the time is right. Meanwhile, you're to cooperate with the enemy."

Kwasind went to his bedroom. Two Hawks lay awake for a while on his own bed. He thought of Horst Raske. The German thought he had this world in his hands. But if the Blodlandish meant to kill Two Hawks if he did side with the Perkunishans, then they must be planning to assassinate Raske. Only by killing him could they deprive the Perkunishans of the superior weapons and technology Raske could provide.

12

THE FOLLOWING WEEK was busy. Each morning, Two Hawks spent three hours with language lessons. After these, he worked until midnight or later in his office. This was in a huge factory on the outskirts of Berlin. He rode to work in a car which was preceded and followed by armored cars. He knew they were there not only to bar his escape but to guard him against assassination.

Raske gave him the task of building a device to synchronize machine-gun fire with the revolutions of an airplane propeller. Two Hawks knew the basic principles. Even so, it took him four days to construct a prototype. His first job done, he then supervised a group working on rockets to be fired from an airplane. This took him a week. After that, he was made head engineer of a group that was designing machines, tools, and techniques for building aircraft on a mass basis.

Two Hawks had only gotten started on this when Raske removed him. The German said, "I have a much more interesting job. You and I are going to train pilots. These will be the nucleus of the Imperial Perkunishan Air Force. How does it feel to be cofounder of an air force?"

Raske glowed with joy. He was always enthusiastic, happy, and optimistic. Two Hawks knew that Raske would have him shot if he thought Two Hawks was a traitor, but he could not help liking Raske. The feeling certainly made it easier to work with, and for, him.

Three weeks passed. Fall came swiftly; winter would soon be here. Two Hawks asked Kwasind if he had received any more messages from the Blodland agents. Kwasind replied, "No. I was told I would not be contacted again until they're ready to act."

Two Hawks did not tell Kwasind that he was not, at the moment, concerned about escape. Despite himself, he was getting enthusiastic about the pilot-training. By then, there were four tandem two-seater monoplanes ready, all hand-built. Each had a rotary, water-cooled, 12-cylinder engine, dual controls, and a range of 150 miles. They could cruise at 100 mph.

They were far from being what Raske could have built if he had had more time and better materials. Aluminum was lacking, and the steel was not even up to the 1918 A.D. standards of Earth 1. The gasoline was low grade. Thus, the airplane had to be of utmost simplicity and confined in speed and range. Still, they were adequate for the present purposes of the Perkunishan Air Force, which were scouting and strafing and bombing of near-front ammunition dumps. And the destruction of dirigibles.

Raske planned on building more rugged and faster pursuit planes later and also hoped to have a force of two-motored bombers. The Perkunishan High Command said that this would have to be much later. It expected to have finished conquest of Europe before these were needed. When the time came to tackle the Ikhwani of South Africa and the Saariset (the Finnic speakers of the Japanese islands of Earth 1), then better and more varied aircraft could be designed.

The day that Raske flew the first one, the Kassandras himself came out with the High Command to observe.

The Perkunishan ruler was a tall, heavily bearded man in his early fifties. He had lost his right arm in the last war when he led an infantry charge against the only Blodlandish fort holding out on the European mainland. During the face-to-face combat that followed, a Blodlandish officer had severed the young officer's arm during a sword-fight. The outraged Perkunishan troops had executed the Blodlandish victor and then massacred all the defenders.

Two Hawks was introduced to the Kassandras. Having been drilled for an hour on the ritual phrases and gestures used during the occasion, he got through it without disgracing himself. The Kassandras had Two Hawks stand by him since he wanted his technical questions answered while Raske was aloft. Raske swaggered out of the hangar. He wore a red, black, and blue uniform he had designed himself as the dress of the new air force. On his head was a helmet with a spike on top, a long yellow scarf was tied around his neck, and he carried a pair of goggles with hexagonal rims.

The Kassandras' daughter, Persinai, went to him, and he put his arm around her waist and kissed her lightly on the cheek. Her father did not seem to mind what they were doing, but some of the noblemen scowled. They belonged to a faction that did not like the princess being in love with a foreigner and, far worse, a commoner. Nor did they like the power he had in military affairs. It was no secret that the head of Internal Security, himself only a lesser nobleman, half-Rasnan, was a very good friend of Raske's.

Raske climbed into the plane and started the engine. This made the High Command gasp, since internal-combustion ground vehicles so far had to be cranked and the dirigible motors had to be turned over by auxiliary steam-engines before starting. The silvery low-wing monoplane took off, climbed to 3,000 feet, and then went through a series of spins, loops, and Immelmans. It came in for a three-point landing. Two Hawks winced at the impact on the rubberless rims of the wheels. While the others clustered around Raske to congratulate him, Two Hawks examined the landing gear. The spokes of the wheels were bent a little. After a few more landings, the wheels would have to be replaced. It would be two or more years before synthetic rubber would be available. The chemists were experimenting on the basis of information from Raske, but he had only a vague idea about the making of neoprene from chloroprene.

The next five days, the German and the American tested out all four prototypes. They also made machine-gun strafing attacks on dummies on the ground, shot rockets, and dropped bombs. Two Hawks noticed that, when he took a plane up, its tank was always only a quarter-full. Raske was taking no chances that his colleague might cut and run for the seacoast, only 90 miles away.

The aircraft factory was working in three shifts at top speed. Despite this, the first mass-produced planes would not be turned out for at least a month. Raske and Two Hawks were up in the air every daylight hour training pilots. When ten had enough skill (not in Two Hawks' estimation), they began to instruct others. The inevitable happened. One plane spun in with both instructor and student. Another stalled during takeoff and was completely demolished, although the pilot suffered only minor injuries.

Raske was furious. "We've only two left. And we're losing time on those, what with repairs and changing wheels!"

Two Hawks shrugged, but he was more concerned than he appeared. He had a plan which required one of the planes. If the accidents continued, he would be grounded for a long time.

One evening, while he was working on a design for auxiliary detachable fuel tanks, Kwasind came into his study.

"Day after tomorrow," he said. "The Blodlandish agent says we must be ready when dusk comes. Just before we leave the airfield to come here."

"What's the plan?"

Kwasind said that the two armored cars which usually accompanied them would be ordered off to deal with a fake emergency. The order would be given by a Blodlandish agent in the uniform of a Kreion (general). After the guards had driven off, Kwasind would kill the soldier that rode with them, and Two Hawks would dispose of the chauffeur. Should the commander of the armored cars refuse to obey the pseudo-kreion's orders, both cars would be bombed and the survivors shot by agents hidden near the field. However, the Blodlandish hoped this would not be necessary.

"Where are they taking us?"

"They'll drive us through the country at night and we'll hide out during the day at various stations. When we get to the coast, a boat will take us to Tyrsland (Sweden). Perkunisha hasn't invaded Tyrsland yet, it isn't strong enough to worry about. In Tyrsland, we'll be flown out by a dirigible to Norway. From there, a ship will take us to Blodland."

"Sounds risky to me," Two Hawks said. "But I guess they know what they are doing."

Raske greeted him as he came into the hangar just after the second of the morning's instruction flights. The German had a peculiar smile. Two Hawks wondered if the escape plot had somehow been exposed. He looked around for arresting officers, but everything seemed normal. The workers were putting together two new planes, the parts for which had been rushed through factories and shipped to the field. A group of students was listening to a lecture by one of the recently graduated aviators. The only soldiers in sight were the usual guards. Nevertheless, he patted the derringer stuck inside his belt to reassure himself that it was there. The Itskapintik police had missed it when they had searched him, they were so eager to get to Ilmika. And the Perkunishans had never searched him because they presumed the Itskapintik had done so.

Raske said, "You once told me you admired the Lady Ilmika. How would you like to have her?"

"What do you mean?" Two Hawks said. He was not sure that Raske was not trying to trap him, although he did not know how an interest in her could do it.

"Don't you know what's happened to her?"

Two Hawks shook his head.

"I don't suppose anybody told you. She's in disgrace; she's in prison. The Kassandras himself offered her her freedom if she would renounce Blodland for allegiance to Perkunisha. The stupid bitch slapped his face! Can you imagine that? Struck the Kassandras in the face and before the entire court! It's a wonder she wasn't executed on the spot! Believe me, His Majesty was angry enough to do it.

"But his wife pleaded for the girl, and the Kassandras merely had her imprisoned. He couldn't stand being humiliated, however, so he's been thinking of some suitable punishment for her."

Raske grinned and continued, "I remembered how you said she was so beautiful, but you'd never be able to touch her. So, my red-skinned friend, just to show what a high regard I have for you, and also how I take care of my own. I've arranged for you to have your heart's desire. I spoke to the Kassandras this morning, and he was delighted. He believes my plan will provide the abasement and the hurt she deserves. And you'll be benefited. I wish I were in your shoes. I'd love to have her for myself. Only I wouldn't dare. The Kassandras' daughter isn't very liberal minded."

"Are you serious?" Two Hawks said.

Raske laughed and said, "The Lady Ilmika, niece to the Milka (king) of Blodland and grandniece to the Kassandras, is yours! She's to be your slave! You have carte blanche with her. I ... What's the matter, *Zwei Habichten*? I thought you'd be delighted. Or are you ... ?"

"Overwhelmed is the word," Two Hawks said. "Only ... Never mind. What happens to her if I don't accept her?"

"Not accept? You must be out of your mind! *Selig*! If you are so insane to reject my offer—well, I don't know. I heard that Ilmika could be placed in solitary until she dies. Or perhaps sent to a military brothel, although I don't really think the Kassandras would do that to his grandniece. Who knows? Who cares?"

Two Hawks should not have cared. But he did. Without

considering the realities and logic of his situation, he knew he had to take Ilmika in as his slave. This was the only way to save her. Her presence would complicate the escape plan. The Blodlandish agents would be furious. Or would they? She was the daughter of a noble and niece to the ruler of their country. Why wouldn't they be glad to include her?

He said, "O.K. Send her over."

Raske clapped him on the shoulder and winked. "Tell me how it works out, heh?"

Two Hawks wanted to hit him but forced himself to unclench his fists and to smile.

"I might do that."

Raske said that they had had enough fun; they must get back to work. Two Hawks would have to handle the aviation school today. Raske had to attend a conference with the head of Ordnance.

"He's the most reactionary and stupid man I ever met," Raske said. "I designed a clip-loaded carbine which will give the infantryman ten times the firepower he now has. Do you think that pighead will accept it? No, he says the common soldier will misuse it; he'll spray the bullets instead of taking careful aim. The carbine will waste ammunition.

"However, that isn't his only reason for not wanting my carbine! Did you know that the gatling gun crews are all officers? No noncoms or privates are allowed to handle a gatling except in extreme emergencies. This ridiculous rule is based on what happened 30 years ago. When Perkunisha was defeated, part of the army and a great number of workers, serfs, and slaves revolted. The uprising was stamped out, but ever since then the aristocracy has made sure the commoner doesn't get his hands on powerful weapons. The rule might have been necessary at one time, but now it's absurd! The swine!"

Two Hawks waited until an hour before dusk to begin the initial stage of his plan. Raske was not likely to come to the field at this late hour, so Two Hawks felt safe. On the pretext that one of the planes had a motor that sounded peculiar, he grounded the plane. Then, as if the thought had suddenly come to him, he announced that he wanted to try an experiment. While some mechanics were trying to locate the source of the "funny noise," others were welding attachments to two gasoline tanks. These, Two Hawks explained, were to be installed on the underside of the wings. The tanks were fitted to the mounting apparatus for the rockets. Hoses were connected to the tanks and run up to the motor's gasoline intake. He supervised the installation of necessary valves. By then, those working on the motor said that they could not locate the supposed trouble. Two Hawks told them to forget about it; he might have been mistaken. He climbed into the cockpit and restarted the motor. The main gas tanks had been drained until they were almost empty. Two Hawks let the motor run for several minutes before turning on the valve to the auxiliary tanks. The motor continued to turn over without a single miss during the switchover.

It was midnight by then. Two Hawks ordered the auxiliaries disconnected and removed. He had the tanks carried back to the hangar rear, where they would be out of Raske's sight. On the way back to the apartment in Berlin, he explained what he had done to Kwasind.

"I want you to get hold of your contact and find out what he intends to do. Tell him the plans have been changed. No, better still, have him talk directly to me. I have to explain in detail what's needed."

Kwasind protested that the Blodlandish would refuse. It was too dangerous to contact Two Hawks personally.

"Tell him if he doesn't, the whole thing's off. Now, when can I meet him?"

"Early tomorrow morning. Before you leave for the airfield, Kwasind said.

When they walked into their suite, they found two soldiers with Ilmika Thorrsstein. She sat on a sofa, her hands folded on her lap, her back straight, her face haughty. Despite her dignity, she looked washed out. The coil of long blonde hair on top of her head was loose, with strands of straying hair, and she wore no makeup. Moreover, she wore a loose-fitting blouse and skirt of cheap dyed cotton, a slave girl's garments.

When she saw Two Hawks enter, he eyes widened and her lips parted. Evidently she had not been told whose apartment this was. Perhaps, she did not know what her lot was to be.

Two Hawks dismissed the soldiers.

She spoke first. "What am I doing here?"

Two Hawks told her bluntly. She took the news without flinching.

"You must be tired and hungry," Two Hawks said. "Kwasind, bring her some food and wine."

"And then?" she said. She gazed steadily at him. He grinned at her until she flushed.

"Not what you think," he said. "I don't want a woman who doesn't desire me. I won't force you."

She looked at the two Kinnukinuk girls, who had just come out of the kitchen.

"What about them?"

"They're slaves. They won't be staying tonight. You can sleep in their room. What's more, you can lock the door on the inside."

Suddenly, tears ran down her cheeks. Her lips quivered. She rose to her feet and then began to sob loudly. He put his arm around her shoulders and pressed her face against his chest. She cried violently for a few minutes before drawing away from him. He gave her a handkerchief to dry her tears. Kwasind appeared and said that her supper was ready in her room. Ilmika, without a word, followed Kwasind.

When the giant had returned, Two Hawks said, "I'll talk to her before she goes to sleep. She has to know what's going on."

"Why are you doing this for her?"

"Maybe I'm in love with her. Or maybe I'm hopelessly chivalric—a red-skinned Gawain. I don't know. I do know I can't just let her be locked up for the rest of her life or be sent to an army whorehouse."

Kwasind shrugged to indicate that he did not understand. But if Two Hawks wanted it that way, so be it.

After a short and unrefreshing sleep, Two Hawks left the bedroom to go to the kitchen. He stopped when he saw a man in the recreation room talking to Kwasind. The stranger wore the blue-and-grey of a servant and carried a bundle of linen. He had long brown hair, a thick brown moustache, and a hawk nose. His name—his real name—was Rulf Andersson.

Two Hawks ordered the two into his room. While Andersson busied himself changing the bedclothes, he talked in a low voice.

"Kwasind told me your plan. You're insane!"

"Would Blodland like to have a brand-new flying machine?" Two Hawks said. "A readymade model the possession of which would cut months off of the designing and building of others? My plan isn't impossible. In fact, it's the very daring, the very unexpectedness of it, that will aid its success."

"I don't know," Andersson said. "It's fantastic."

"Can you get in touch with your compatriots in Tyrsland?"

"Yes. But to set up what you want, we need a few days."

"No extra time," Two Hawks said. "Raske is bound to notice the auxiliaries sooner or later. Or somebody will tell him about them. We have to move fast. Day after tomorrow, the latest."

"All right, we'll do it. I'll see Kwasind later, and he'll tell you if we'll be able to make it."

Two Hawks explained his plan in detail and made sure that Andersson knew exactly what was required. The agent left. Two Hawks tried the door to Ilmika's room. It was locked.

"Kwasind, you stay here today. We have to pretend we are going along with the idea she's my slave. So you make her do some work here, dust, cook, and so on. Get her some makeup and pretty clothes. I wouldn't want my slave mistress to be unattractive, would I?"

He left for the airfield. He was busy that day, since he also had to do Raske's work. The German was at a conference with the High Command. This was fine with Two Hawks. He did more work on the auxiliary tanks and then took the plane up for a flight test of the apparatus. After landing, he was met by the officer in charge of assembling two planes in the rear of the hangar. The officer told him that the planes were ready for installation of their gas tanks. The auxiliaries would have to be removed from the plane and the attachments cut off. He was sorry, but there were no other tanks on hand to use.

"Very well," Two Hawks said. "Do it tomorrow."

"But Raske ordered that the planes be assembled without delay. The second and third shifts can install the tanks tonight."

Scowling, Two Hawks spoke harshly.

"I want Raske to see my auxiliaries. They'll extend the range of our planes by a hundred miles. No, this is far more important than a day's holdup on those machines. I order you to leave those gas tanks alone."

"My men won't have anything to do! Raske will hold me responsible for the delay!"

"I'll take full responsibility," Two Hawks said. "You and your men take the night off. You've been working too hard. I'll sign the order for a night's leave."

The officer seemed reluctant, but he saluted and then

walked off to tell the others the new orders. Two Hawks
watched him. There was a chance the officer might phone
Raske to get verification of the change. If Raske heard of this,
he would guess at once what the American meant to do.

Two Hawks went after the officer.

"You seem to be worrying that you may get into trouble,"
he said. "I suggest you call Raske now. If he orders you to
continue work, then do so. I will still be responsible for any
delay up to the moment you get into contact with him."

The officer brightened. He hastened away, only to return
in ten minutes with a frustrated expression. "He is in conference. He refused to talk to me but did send word that if
I had any problems, I was to go to you."

"So, you see, you have no more responsibility."

Two Hawks breathed easier; his gamble had paid off.

Kwasind met Two Hawks the moment he walked into the
suite.

"Andersson says that the agents in Tyrsland have been informed about the change in plans. And the agents at the
emergency field are ready, just in case. Andersson can't tell
us any more until tomorrow morning. But he's very worried.
If the winds along the coast are too strong, the plane can't be
gotten out."

"In that case, we'll have to forget about the plane and take
the fishing boat," Two Hawks said. "Where's Ilmika?"

"She just went into her room."

Two Hawks knocked at her door. It swung open to reveal
a different woman—on the outside, anyway. Her Psyche knot
was flawless, her eyes were made up, and her lips rouged.
She was wearing a Neo-Cretan gown, cut low in front, a
golden belt tight around her waist, and a hoop skirt with a
broad V in front which showed a rich silk petticoat.

"Her Ladyship looks beautiful," he said. "However, you'll
have to change into something less attractive but more
durable and unrestraining. Can you look like a Perkunishan
soldier?"

She laughed and said, "I've been cutting and sewing all
day to refit one of your uniforms."

Seeing him raise his eyebrows, she said, "Blodlandish
laides have slaves or servants to do the work, but they're
still taught all the domestic arts. How can we properly educate
and supervise our slaves if we know nothing ourselves?"

"That seems sensible," he replied. He had much to say

about slavery, most of it condemnation. This was, however, n[ ]
time for discussion.

"We'll leave early enough to get to the airfield before day
break. I've purposely not held to a rigid schedule, so there'[ ]
be no suspicions about variations in departure."

She looked so fresh and beautiful that he wanted to kis[ ]
her. He restrained the impulse, knowing that she would b[ ]
offended. Even if she were attracted to him, she could show
no more affection towards him than towards any faithful serv[ ]
ant or devoted commoner.

He said goodnight to her and went to bed. He fell asleep
at once and, it seemed a minute later, was being shaken b[ ]
Kwasind.

"It can't be time yet?"

"No. You'e wanted on the phone. It's Raske."

"At this hour?" By the dim light of the gas jet, he looke[ ]
at the clock on the bedside table. It was 2 a.m.

"What the hell can he want?"

Kwasind said, "I don't know. I hope nothing's wrong."

Two Hawks lurched into the next room and picked up th[ ]
phone. There was a hiss and crackle on the line, and Raske'[ ]
voice sounded a little blurred. The Perkunishan system o[ ]
reproducing voice left much to be desired.

"Raske?"

"Two Hawks!" Raske exploded. "What're you trying t[ ]
pull? As if I didn't know! You ought to be smarter tha[ ]
that, my Indian friend!"

Two Hawks said, "What are you talking about?"

Raske told him. It was as Two Hawks had feared. Th[ ]
worrywart in charge of assembly had not been reassure[ ]
enough. After agonizing for a long time, he had tried agai[ ]
to get hold of Raske. This time, he succeeded in reaching
the German, who was at a party given by the Kassandras[ ]
wife. As soon as Raske was told about the auxiliaries, he ha[ ]
guessed Two Hawks' purpose.

"I'm not going to say anything to anybody about this,[ ]
Raske said. "I like you. What's more important, I need you[ ]
So you're getting off easily. But you're going to have les[ ]
freedom. You'll follow a schedule to the minute; I'll kno[ ]
where you are and what you're doing every second of th[ ]
day and night."

Raske paused. Two Hawks did not reply. With a slightl[ ]
palintive tone, the German resumed.

"Why do you want to run off? You've got it made here. Blodland can't give you a thing. Besides, Blodland is doomed. It'll be comquered by this time next year."

"I'm just not sympatico with the Perkunishans," Two Hawks said. "They remind me of the Germans too much."

"You red-skinned swine!"

Raske stopped again. Two Hawks could hear him breathing heavily. Then, "One more trick, and you go to the firing quad! Or to the torture chamber! Do you understand me?"

"I get you," Two Hawks said. "Anything else? I want to get back to bed."

Surprisingly, Raske laughed. "You're a cool one. I like that. Very well. You will leave your suite at exactly 6 a.m. and will report to the airfield commander as soon as you arrive. Moreover, your slave, Kwasind, is to be restricted to the suite. I'll notify your guards at once. Another thing. If you don't behave, your little blonde playmate will be taken away. Got it?"

"Got it," Two Hawks said. He hung up.

13

HE REPEATED RASKE'S conversation to Kwasind. The giant listened without change of expression. He said, "What now?"

"It's now or never. We can't go out the front way, so we'll use the back."

Kwasind looked puzzled. Two Hawks said, "Out the window. You try playing Hercules with the steel bars of my bedroom window. I'll wake Ilmika."

Five minutes later, he and Ilmika entered his bedroom. She was in the uniform of an officer of the Perkunisha Imperial Air Force. Her cap sat snugly on her head, since she had cut off her long hair.

Kwasind had torn one bar out of its stone socket and was bending another. The two watched him in awe. Slowly, the inch-thick steel curved. Kwasind, face impassive and free of strain, feet braced against the wall, pulled. Just before the separation of the bar ends from the stone, he lowered his feet to the floor. Now the lower part of his body was against the wall, and the upper part bowed outwards. Screeching, the steel tore loose. Kwasind caught himself, bent his knees, half turned. He placed the bar on the carpet and grinned.

"We can squeeze through now."

They cut strips from the bedsheets and knotted the ends together. They had just enough material to make a strong double-thick rope which reached from the third-story window to about five feet from the ground. Two Hawks scanned the broad street and sidewalk below. There was no one in sight. However, he knew that a sentinel was stationed at the north exit, to their right. He was on the other side of a massive pillar. Unless he stepped out onto the great portico, he would not see the white ribbon hanging along the outer wall.

"Stick that bar in your belt," Two Hawks said to Kwasind. "I'll take the other. We might need them."

He went through the window first. He slid out withou

hesitation, having tested the security of the knot at the upper end. This was tied to a bedpost. Hand under hand, he descended swiftly. When he dropped to the ground, he looked around. No one had appeared on the street yet. Ilmika followed him a minute later, then, Kwasind.

Two Hawks led them down the street, away from the guard at the north door. He wanted a car, but they walked four long blocks—over a mile—before they found one. Rather, it almost found them. A glare of headlights from a sidestreet warned them just in time. They ran into a deep doorway and pressed against the door to be as far as possible in the shadow. Two Hawks decided he would have to risk a peek. The car sounded as if it were traveling slowly enough for him to run up to it and jump upon the running board.

He looked and saw the white body of a topless car and the image of a knight in armor with raised sword on its hood. It was a police car with three men in it. He told Kwasind what to do. Both had the bars in their hands. The hood of the vehicle drew even with the doorway. Two Hawks said, "Now!" He ran out with the bar held slantwise in front of him, Kwasind even with him.

The patrolmen had been talking. They stopped, rigid and speechless for a second with surprise. Then the driver slammed on the brakes when he should have stepped on the accelerator. Two Hawks leaped up into the top of the rear door and hurled himself at the man sitting in the rear seat. He swung the steel bar as he did so. The patrolman stood up and raised his rifle to parry the blow. There was a clang as the bar drove against the gun barrel. Both fell on the seat with Two Hawks on top.

Two Hawks, using the bar as a sword, jammed its end into the man's mouth. A rifle exploded, almost in his ear, but if it had been aimed at him it had missed.

The patrolman's teeth broke. Two Hawks got to a kneeling position on the man's chest and leaned his weight on the bar. It entered the throat, and, despite the frenzied efforts of the patolman to push it out, remained there. His eyes bulged; his face darkened. Suddenly, he quit struggling.

Two Hawks held the bar until he was certain the man was dead. He rose, took the bar out, and turned his attention to the others. Kwasind had no need of him. The driver was lying on his side on the seat, his neck was broken by a blow from Kwasind's bar. The other, the man who had fired the

rifle, had been knocked out of the car. He, too, was dead
strangled by Kwasind.

"You hit?" Two Hawks said.

"His rifle went off as I knocked it downwards," Kwasind
said. "I'm all right."

Two Hawks looked up and down the street. If anyone had
heard the gunfire, they were making no outcry about it. He
dragged the corpse off the back seat and onto the pavement
While he restarted the motor and became acquainted with the
controls, Kwasind dragged all three bodies into the doorway
A few minutes later, armed with revolvers and single-shot
rifles, they drove off. Two Hawks followed the route taken
to the airfield every morning. Twice, they passed patrol cars
going the other way. The drivers tooted at them, Two Hawks
tooted back, and that was all. Two Hawks asked Kwasind if
he knew where the Blodlandish agents were located. He had
some hope that they could be used to make a diversion, as
originally planned. Kwasind replied that his contact had refused to give him that information.

"Then we'll have to do this by ourselves—The Lonesome
Three. The only trouble is, we're way ahead of schedule
I'll bet that worrywart officer went back to the hangar and
had the auxiliary tanks removed. That means we'll have to
land once to refuel before we get to the coast. If the Blodlandish don't have the gas ready, we're screwed."

"Maybe we ought to worry about getting into the air first,"
Kwasind said. Two Hawks glanced at him. The panel light
showed him the giant's usual stolid expression. However
his face gleamed with sweat. Two Hawks smiled. He doubted
that the perspiration was caused by exertions or nervousness
from the fight with the patrolmen. Kwasind had been more
than uneasy when told how they would escape. Brave and
cool in combat on the ground, he was terrified at the idea of
flying. He had not said so, but his questions and a rigidity
whenever the subject came up betrayed him.

There was, however, more to his nervous state than just
the concept of leaving the ground. The ancient European
religions had been heavy with stories of flying demons. The
new religion of Hemilkism discredited these as mere superstitions. Old horrors die hard; at least half of the population
firmly believed in the demons. And Kwasind was a member
of one of the old religions which had not died. It thrived
in underground form in his oppressed country. Even now

thinking of the winged monsters, Kwasind must be hearing the beat of their wings.

Leaving Berlin proper, they drove on a broad highway through the suburbs. A ten minutes' traffic-free drive through these and five minutes of speeding through farmland brought them to the airfield. This was completely encircled by a thirty-foot high barbed wire fence. Dogs much like German shepherds patrolled the fence at nights. There was no way of entrance except through the main gate. They would have to brazen through.

Two Hawks stopped the car in response to a guard's order. The other guard remained by the sentinel box, his rifle ready, while the first walked up to the car.

"Pulkininkas (Colonel) Two Hawks and party," Two Hawks said. He spoke as if he had great authority. The soldier was hesitant. Finally, he said, "Where is your body-guard, Colonel?"

He looked at the car and his eyes widened. "This is a police car!"

Two Hawks raised his revolver and shot the guard in the solar plexus. The guard fell backwards, and Two Hawks shot him again. Kwasind had raised his rifle at the same time. He fired just above Two Hawks' head, deafening him. The guard by the box had lifted his rifle to fire at them, but he was too slow. Kwasind's first bullet turned him 180 degrees around. Kwasind dropped the rifle and pulled his revolver from its holster. By then, Ilmika had hit the guard with a bullet from her revolver.

Kwasind jumped out of the car and removed from the dead sergeant's belt a ring full of keys. He tried four keys before he found the proper one to unlock the big padlock on the wire gate. Ilmika collected the sentries' rifles and cartridge belts and put them in the back seat.

Kwasind opened the gates. Two Hawks eased the car through to give the giant a chance to get back into the car. Shouts rose from the barracks near the rear of the hangar. A man with a revolver ran out of the officers' quarters. Two Hawks pressed down on the accelerator. The officer ran after them, shouting. His revolver cracked. Half-dressed soldiers with rifles ran out of the barracks.

The car hurtled around the corner of the hangar, then skidded as Two Hawks tapped on the brakes. He straightened it out, made a sharp right turn, and wheeled it through the doorless front of the hangar. He stopped the car with a squeal of brakes and tires by the airplane titled *Raske II*. Kwasind jumped out and ran back to the corner of the building, where he began firing at those who had been chasing them.

The workers assembling the two planes in the rear had stopped work when the car had roared in. Two Hawks shot once over their heads. They did not wait for a second bullet but fled to the exit in the rear. Ilmika took a position behind an empty barrel to shoot at the first soldier to enter the rear door.

Two Hawks swore when he looked a the *Raske II*. The auxiliaries and their attachments had been removed. He shrugged and said, *"C'est la guerre,"* put on his helmet and climbed into the monoplane. He turned on the valves and switches. At least, the tanks were full, and the machine guns had a full supply of ammunition.

He pressed on the starter. There was a whining noise. The wooden propeller turned over slowly at first, then more swiftly as the motor coughed as if speed were stuck in its throat.

Kwasind and Ilmika left their posts to run for the plane. She climbed into the rear cockpit. Kwasind stopped at a signal from Two Hawks and stepped up onto the wing so he could hear Two Hawks. He grinned, climbed back down, and removed the chocks from the wheels.

Two Hawks gave the motor more gas and turned the rudder a hard right. The plane described a half-circle to face the *Raske I*. Kwasind got under the tail of the *Raske II* and lifted. When the fuselage was parallel to the floor, Two Hawks began firing the twin machine guns. The other plane shivered under the impact as big holes appeared in its fabric in a line that sped towards the gas tanks as Kwasind continued to move the fuselage.

The *Raske I* exploded. Dense smoke spread through the hangar and set Two Hawks and Ilmika to coughing. He felt the heat from the blaze. Fortunately, the *Raske I* had been at the other wall of the hangar, some hundred yards away. Even so, Two Hawks had not been sure that the flaming gas would not spread out to his own plane. He had to take the chance, because he did not want anybody pursuing him. Overloaded with three people, he would be too slow and awkward to dogfight the *Raske I*. And he did not have time to destroy the plane any other way.

The plane continued to pivot as the giant moved its tail. Two Hawks fired again while the nose described a horizontal arc. The smoke was so thick that he could not see whether or not the soldiers had left the protection of the other side of the hangar wall. If they had tried to rush through the smoke, they would have been caught in the fire from the machine guns. Similarly, any troops entering the rear door should have been discouraged by the hail of lead.

Kwasind continued to carry the tail around until the plane was facing the entrance.

Two Hawks held the brakes until Kwasind had squeezed in beside Ilmika. The giant's face was rigid. Two Hawks looked back, grinned at him, released the brakes, and pulled the throttle out. The plane jumped like a frightened rabbit; his head was driven back into the headrest. The *Raske II* roared out into the firelit night. Soldiers ran out from behind the hangar walls and shot at the plane. A bullet tore a hole in the fabric of the cockpit on his right.

The tail lifted, but the wheels clung to the ground. There was more weight than the craft was designed to normally carry. For what seemed like a deadly long time, the plane refused to rise. The end of the paved strip shot up; beyond was a hundred yards of earth and then a thirty-foot high fence.

Two Hawks waited until the plane had bumped over fifty yards of grass. By then, the wheels were a few inches off the ground. He pulled back on the stick, and they left the earth and passed over the fence with six inches to spare. Past the fence was a copse of trees, the tips of which brushed against the wheels. Two Hawks breathed out relief and continued the climb. Now he would head northward until dawn gave him enough visibility to get his bearings. He wished there had been enough time to attach the auxiliary tanks. This would have made the emergency landing at the halfway point unnecessary.

Then it occurred to him that the extra weight of the auxiliary tanks would have sent them into the fence. He could have tried taking off to the north, where the field was longer, but he would have been in a crosswind. Moreover, taxiing down to the south end would have given the Perkunishans a chance to go after him in cars. No, things had worked out much better this way. The whole crazy way.

Improvisation is my forte, Two Hawks said to himself. He sang a Seneca warchant his mother had taught him and then some lines from The Vagabond King. Kwasind was rigid, head bent down. Daylight came. Two Hawks talked to him through the earphones. Kwasind said he felt sick. Looking at anything but the cockpit floor made him want to vomit. His knees were turned to water, and he was curling inside like a pillar of smoke.

Ilmika, however, was thrilled. She exclaimed with joy as they passed over houses and barns a thousand feet below, and she pointed like a delighted child at the tiny people and cows. Two Hawks, as the sun climbed, lost his exultation. The fuel indicator was dropping faster than he had hoped. He was also worried about the earliness of their arrival at the refueling point—if they got there. Should the Blodland agents in Berlin not find out about the escape soon enough, they would not notify the agents at the farm near Gervuoge. And then there was the possibility that the agents at Gervuoge had been discovered, and that Perkunishans would be waiting for the plane when it landed.

Two Hawks groaned, but a little while later laughed at himself. Oh, God! The mighty Iroquois warrior one minute and the next a big worrywart. So something goes wrong. I've been doing all right so far by playing it by ear.

Their second landing, the last to be made in Perkunishan territory, was to be on the Baltic Sea coast. This stretch of shoreline was the northernmost reach of a peninsula that was on Earth 1, if Two Hawks remembered his geography correctly, the island of Rügen. Since the glacial conditions of this world had locked up so much water in ice, the Baltic Sea was smaller than on Earth 1. Thus, the island had become a peninsula, and the southern Baltic coastline extended further north.

After landing on this coast, the refugees were supposed to be picked up by a Blodlandish dirigible from the island of Aabryg. On Earth 1, this island was Bornholm and was Danish territory. Here, Aabryg belonged to Tyrsland, Earth 2's equivalent of Sweden. The dirigible was to transport Two Hawks and party and the plane, if it could be managed, to Aabryg, then to Tyrsland, then to Norway and thence to Blodland.

By the time he had reached the southern shore of the large lake of Ramumas, the gas indicator had just reached empty. This meant he had one gallon left. Not much to fly around on while he looked for the farm. For one thing, he was too far to the east, or thought he was. Going west, he had to beat against a strong headwind, which was eating up his precious gallon just that much faster.

Come on, you limeys, he prayed. He passed over a crossroads in the form of a Celtic cross and knew he was three miles from the assignation point. There should be another dirt road two miles westward, then a little peninsula in the form of a question mark. A half mile past it should be a farm isolated from two others by a quarter-mile stretch of woods. The roof of the barn would be painted with two interlocking triskelions, the three-limbed symbols that were on the national flag of the six kingdoms that originally comprised the empire of Blodland. If it was all right for him to land, he would see two rocket flares. If not, he would see nothing, except maybe a troop of Perkunishans waiting for him. In either case, he would have to land, he was so low on gas.

The farm came into sight as they passed over a high hill. Ilmika jabbed her forefinger below and smiled. Just ahead was a lare white barn with two red interlocking triskelions on one side of its sloping roof. He circled over the farm, searching the ground and also waiting to hear the sputter of motor. Three times he went around, coming lower each time. If the signals did not come, he would try to get past the woods to the farm on its other side. At least, they would have a headstart on their pursuers, although a successful escape seemed unlikely. But the Perkunishans would get a run for their bloodmoney.

Three men came out of the barn. Two held up tubes which glittered in the sun. Each tube spat a dark object up to a height of thirty feet, at which the flares burst into a red and a green.

The landing could have been easy, since a long and broad meadow with a flat surface offered itself. However, a split-log fence bisected the meadow. Two Hawks had to sideslip to lose altitude fast enough and then gauge his glide path so he barely cleared the fence. The plane stopped with its nose not a foot from the edge of the woods. After taxiing back to the fence, he cut the motor and climbed out. Six men and a woman, all dressed in the coarse brown homespun of peasants, were waiting for him.

The introductions were short. Aelfred Hennend, the leader, said, "We got word by wireless just in time." He gave an order, and the other men left to get the gas and oil. Two Hawks said, "The fence has to be broken down if we're to have enough runway." Hennend replied that that would be done. He invited them into the house for some food and coffee. On the way he said, "Our neighbors may come nosing around. Your flying machine is bound to make them excited. There may even be troops on the way. We'll have to disappear just as soon as your machine is fueled. Too bad, too. Hate to give up this place, it's a good station for our underground. But if you can deliver that contraption to Blodland, the sacrifice will be worth it."

Two Hawks did not apologize. While he ate, he asked Hennend about the next landing. He went over a map with him. A radio operator came in to say that the weather on the Baltic coast was all right. There was an overcast but no promise of rain, and the wind was moderate. Also, the *lyftship*, the dirigible, was on its way from Tyrsland.

Two Hawks returned to the plane to supervise the refueling. The fence had been taken apart in the middle for a distance of fifty feet. The oxen and the cart that had brought barrels of gas were by the plane. The tanks were filled in twenty minutes, even though the fuel had to be poured in by hand.

He considered removing the machine guns from the plane. The loss of weight would aid their takeoff and also cut down on fuel consumption. But he had enough leeway in fuel; it would be better to keep the weapons. The Blodlandish would not only have an aircraft as a model but would also have the guns as prototypes.

The two male fliers shook the agents' hands; Ilmika extended her hand to be kissed. They bade the agents godspeed and got into the cockpits. Two Hawks grinned when he saw Kwasind's reluctance. Kwasind had made no attempt to hide his great joy at returning to earth safely. Two Hawks felt sure that Kwasind would stay behind and try to get to Tyrsland via the underground if Two Hawks were to suggest the idea. Perhaps this was a good idea. Without Kwasind, the range and speed of the plane would be much improved.

No, let him suffer now. The sooner he got out of the country, the better. He was so obviously an Indian, he would have a difficult time traveling by day. If he were to be caught, he would be on Two Hawks' conscience. Besides, he was fond of Kwasind.

The takeoff was easy, although Kwasind might not think

o, since the wheels cleared the treetops by ten feet. To Two Hawks, ten feet was as good as a hundred. He climbed to 500 and leveled off. Their destination was an isolated but reasonably smooth beach on the Baltic Sea. Two Hawks located the highway Hennend had marked in red on the map and followed it northward. When he saw the seaport of Saldus at its end, he turned east. Saldus was a city of about 40,000 civilians with 10,000 sailors. There were warships in the harbor and an airship field at the outskirts, but he saw no dirigibles.

Ten miles to the east of Saldus, the land sloped upwards to become a series of rocky cliffs. After two miles of these, he saw the beach. A group of men was standing at one end, and a quarter-mile out was a two-masted fishing boat. Two Hawks made the landing, which was bumpier than he liked, with a hundred feet to spare before the cliffs began again. Even so, he had to sideslip to drop altitude swiftly just as he had done on the previous landing. As soon as he got out of the plane, he checked the landing gear. The wire spokes of the wheels were bent but not enough to worry about. Besides, if the plan went well, neither they nor the cliffs would be a problem.

He talked with agents, who enlightened him on the progress of the war. From the Perkunishan viewpoint, it was progress. From the Blodlandish viewpoint, it was disaster. Perkunisha had completely overrun Dakota, Gotsland, Neftroia, and the eastern half of Hotinohsonih. They had occupied the northern part of Rasna (Earth 1's France and Belgium) but had bogged down in the conquest of the southern half. From Gotsland, the Perkunishan armies had overrun Akhaivia (Italy of Earth 1) as far as Wesperos (Florence). It was expected, from the way things were going, that Akhaivia, Doria (Jugoslavia), and Hatti (Greece) would be occupied within a month or two. The Perkunishan fleet dominated the Mediterranean, since the Shofet of New Crete (the Iberian peninsula) had permitted the fleet to steam through the straits of Herakles (Gibraltar).

A large fleet of Perkunishan airships had defeated a Blodlandish fleet over the Narwe Lagu (English Channel). Another fleet had bombed the city of Bammu (London). So far, the surface navies of the two nations had not had a full-scale battle. However, the Perkinushan navy was somewhat larger than the Blodlandish. There would be a showdown soon, an invasion army was being assembled on the Rasnan coast. The present air superiority of Perkunisha could tip the balance in a naval clash. A dirigible had already sunk a Blodlandish dreadnaught.

Stunning news had come in just that morning. The Shofet of New Crete had decided to jump into the war on the winning side. New Crete had long had a claim on southeastern Ireland and Cornwall, taken from them by the Blodlandish several hundred years ago. Espionage reported that the Shofet and Kassandras had met and agreed that New Crete would get their ancient possessions back. But first, the isles had to be invaded.

The withdrawal of the Blodlandish fleet from the Dravidian (Indian) bases to aid in the defense of the homeland had been an invitation to the Saariset. The semi-caucasoid Finnic-speakers of Saariset (Earth 1's Japanese islands) had launched their navies towards Dravidia. This would make Perkunisha angry, of course, because they intended to add the rich sub-continent to their empire. At the moment, Perkunisha could do nothing about it.

"What about the Ikhwan?" Two Hawks said, referring to the Arabic nation of southern Africa.

"They're not declaring war, just making war. Their armies are marching into both Perkunishan and our African colonies. Moreover, part of their fleet and a host of troop ships are hastening to western Dravidia to reclaim it. We took it away from them, you know."

"Both Earths are in a mess," Two Hawks said. "As usual. Have you heard of any reaction from our escape in Berlin?"

Erik Shop, the chief, said that he had heard nothing. A man interrupted them to report that the dirigible from Tyrsland was sighted. Two Hawks turned to see a small object on the horizon to the seawards. A second later, a shadow fell on them, and the hum of faroff propellers came to them. They looked up. Another airship, its silvery side marked with a black boar's head, was above them. It was going northward at a speed of fifty miles an hour and at an altitude of 500 feet.

Shop swore. "Perkunishan, Mammoth class!"

Two Hawks said, "What chance does your ship have against that monster?"

"The *Guthhavok* is only a light cruiser," Shop replied. He was pale. "Can you fly across the Baltic to Tyrsland?"

"I'd never make it." He looked at the huge airship, shrugged, and said, "There's only one thing to do, like it or not."

14

HE STRODE TO the plane, the tank of which had been refilled in case just such an emergency happened. He asked Shop some questions about airships and then got into the cockpit. He started the motor and taxied down to the extreme end of the beach. The men, who had run after him, held onto the wings while he put his brakes on and then revved the motor up as far as it would go and still not move the plane.

The others had run after him, so he was able to call Ilmika to his side. Above the roar of the motor, he shouted, "If I don't get back, you and Kwasind leave on the fishing boat with the others! They'll get you home!"

Ilmika reached up and pulled his head down and kissed him.

"You're a brave man. Two Hawks! I haven't told you that because I was too proud! After all. . . !"

"I don't have blue blood, and I'm a red-skinned Hotin-ohsonih," he said. "Thanks, anyway! I know what it took for you to bend your stiff Blodlandish neck!"

She must not have heard his final words, since she smiled at him. Then she was busy hanging on to the wing, working with the others to hold the plane down while he held his brakes and sped up the motor. He chopped his hand down, the men let loose of the wings, he released the brakes, and the *Raske II* shot forward. It sped down the beach, bumping, lifted and climbed as steeply upwards as he dared direct it. The black cliffs rushed towards him. He could not clear them if he continued straight ahead, but he could make a sharp bank to the left. He was on his side, the waves directly below him. Then the plane righted, and he began to climb. The throttle was all the way out, since it did not matter how much gas he used.

The long sinister shape of the dirigible, small at first, grew larger. Even though it had a headstart, its top speed was 55 mph; his, 120. The Blodlandish airship had not turned tail. It was continuing straight towards its larger and more heavily armed foe.

Brave but foolhardy. Yet he had to admire them. They had a duty to perform, and if it involved battling an enemy that had them hopelessly outclassed, they would not shirk. The Blodlandish, despite many dissimilarities to their counterparts of Earth 1, resembled them in courage and stubbornness.

The airships were a half-mile apart when Two Hawks caught up with the Perkunishan. He began climbing to get above it, noting as he did so its nomenclature painted in black letters on its side. *Pilkas Tigras. The Grey Tiger.* Mammoth Three Class. There were square windows above the letters. From them came barrels, followed by needles of flame. The fabric on his right wing ripped as several bullets tore through it. He pulled away, seeing at the same time a rocket soaring towards him. It passed fifty feet in front of his nose and exploded. The shock wave rocked the plane; some fragments hurtled by it.

Two Hawks continued to climb while four more rockets exploded around him. Shrapnel or case fragments stitched the side of his cockpit, but the energy was spent and they did not get entirely through the fabric and thin wood. He attained his desired height of three hundred feet above the dirigible and turned. He dived, his angle of descent 45 degrees, then 60. Black squares in the forward upper skin of the airship flicked out little red tongues. Two rockets raced each other to get to him first. Both passed above him and blew up behind him.

When he was five hundred feet away, he fired his twin machine-guns. He kept firing until he was so close he had to veer away or crash into the airship. As he turned, he felt, then heard, the explosion. He looked back and up, since he was now past and below the ship. The center part was wrapped in flames. Quickly, the fire spread throughout the great craft. It settled slowly towards the sea while blue dolls —men—fell from it. They preferred a swift fall and a quick painless death against the hard waters to burning.

Two Hawks leveled off and watched while the *Grey Tiger* sank past him, its stern high, its nose down. It crashed into the sea, and, still flaming, broke up, the light wooden skeleton shattering on impact.

Four minutes later, the *Grey Tiger* was gone. Only some large spiral pieces of wood, a few sections of fabric, and little islands of burning oil were left. He returned to the beach and landed. Ilmika embraced him while the others danced and laughed. He should have felt exultant. He was the victor of a historic event, the first battle in this world between an airship and an airplane. But the sight of the men leaping from the doomed *Grey Tiger*, some with their uniforms blazing, had dampened him. He had too much imagination, or too much empathy, not to feel some of their terror. He had been close to that time of not-to-be-avoided and utter end too many times himself.

The *Guthhavok*, the Blodlandish cruiser, approached the airplane upwind and at a height of fifty feet. The wind was about eight mph and steady, and the big craft did not bob enough to cause Two Hawks concern. When the dirigible was directly above, it lowered a net on the end of a cable from an opening in its belly. The net was spread out on the beach, and the plane was pushed over it. After the net had been lifted up and wrapped around the plane, Two Hawks signalled the airship to start hauling up the cable. The dirigible, tempering the thrust of its propellers to the wind, hovered in one spot. There was an unavoidable jerk when the cable first lifted. Then the plane was rising smoothly, its nose pointing downward because of the weight of the motor, yet so securely wrapped in the net that it did not slip through. The pressure of the net might crush the plane a little, but Two Hawks did not worry about that. It could be repaired when he got to Blodland.

The plane disappeared into the belly of the aerial whale. A few minutes later, the cable was let down again. A large basket, probably taken from an observation balloon for this trip, was at the end of the cable. Ilmika, Kwasind, and Two Hawks climbed into it, grabbed the supporting ropes, and the basket was lifted. The dirigible began rising and at the same time turning northwards. Before the three were inside the airship, it had begun its journey across the sea to Tyrsland.

The basket went up through the hole and was swung to one side, away from the port and onto a small platform. They climbed out with a feeling of relief. An officer conducted them down a catwalk which ran above the longitudinal axis of the *lyftship*. Two Hawks stared at the perforated spiraling wooden frames and the huge spherical cells containing hydrogen. The officer, answering his questions, said that the cell coverings were made of goldbeater's skin. Two Hawks had thought that they would be made of this material, since a rubberized fabric in a world without rubber would be impossible. And so far no one had invented synthetic rubber. He was no chemist, but he could give the scientists enough hints for them to begin research. This world needed him far more than his native world, he thought. The only trouble was, he needed his native world far more than he needed this one. There was no winning. Just fighting.

With which unhappy but not unendurable thought he went down through the port and down a slidepole into the gondola, the bridge. There the *heretoga* (captain) and his chief officers were introduced to the new passengers. Two Hawks was congratulated on his victory over the Perkunishan airship. The heretoga went up with Two Hawks to look at the plane, the exit being made on a very steep and narrow staircase and two handropes. Aethelstan, the captain, was not as jubilant about the plane as he should have been. Two Hawks was puzzled at first, then began to understand. Aethelstan loved his command; he loved the great gas-borne ships. And in this fragile little machine nestling inside the airship like a baby bird in its nest, he saw doom. When enough heavier-than-air machines were built, they would sweep the dirigibles out of the sky. His career would soon be over. He could either go back to surface ships or learn to fly a dangerous and unfamiliar machine, and for the latter, he was too old.

There would be many like him. The war would bring on changes, like all wars, and men would find themselves deprived of that for which they were fitted and which they loved. And the introduction of Raske and Two Hawks into this world was a catalyst to precipitate change even faster than it would normally have occurred and in a far stranger fashion.

Three days later, the three were in Bammu, the capital city of the empire of Blodland. Bammu was on the same site as the London of Earth 1. It had been founded by New Cretan traders who had renamed the Celtic village Bab Mu—the gate of the river. The city was not as large as its Earth 1 counterpart, having only a population of 750,000, including suburbs. The architecture of buildings was more like the city of the 12th century of Earth 1, in Two Hawks' eyes, anyway. The business and government buildings had an alien flavor, a vaguely Levantine impression. Indeed, the west Semitic influence of the New Cretan colonizers was very strong. Many street names were of Cretan origin. The Blodlandish equivalent of Earth 1's parliament, the Witenayemot, was a mixture of Oriental and Nordic elements. Even the king was not called by the old Germanic title; he was the Shof, derived from Shofet, the Cretan word for ruler.

Two Hawks went through a period of interrogation, one very different from that in Hotinohsonih because the Blodlandish knew his value. It was only a week after he had begun making plans for an aircraft plant that he was given a rank of minor nobility. At an evening ceremony, the Shof made him a lord of the realm, the Aetheling of Fenhop. He became the owner of a castle and a number of farms in the north country, near the border of Norland (Scotland of Earth 1). In Bammu itself, he had a small mansion and a number of slaves and servants.

Two Hawks asked Ilmika about the former owners. "The Huskarl of Fenhop was a heretic," she said. "He was hung about thirty years ago, not for heresy but for murdering one of his slaves. If he had not been a heretic, he would have gotten only a large fine and a small jail sentence. His sons migrated to Dravidia, and the property reverted to the crown."

"And now that I am a nobleman," he said, "does that mean I can marry a woman of the nobility?"

Her face reddened. She said, "Oh, no, your patent is to be held by you while you live and is cancelled when you die. Your property goes back to the crown. Your children will be commoners. And you can't marry a noblewoman."

"So my blood isn't good enough to mingle with Blodlandish blood?" he said. "And my children, after being accustomed to the high life, can go begging. From castle to cabin for them, right?"

Ilmika was indignant. "Would you have us be adulterated? Why, the purity of the ancient Blodlandish nobles would be sullied! Our children would be mongrels. Isn't it enough for you that you're a peer of the realm, even if. . . ?"

"Say it, Ilmika Thorrsstein! Even if I'm an outlander and a red-skinned savage, that's what you didn't have enough guts to say, right?"

He spoke two words of ancient Germanic lineage and walked away. He felt an anger that had carried him to the point of striking her. Almost. It was anger that had deeper roots than reaction to being regarded as a mongrel. He knew that he had had some hope—however slight—that Ilmika might be his wife. Damn it! He was in love with a cold-hearted, superstitious, bigoted, illiterate, emotionally stupid, patrician snob! Damn it and damn her! He would do what he should have done at the very beginning! He would forget her.

Yet, she was the one who had praised his courage, valor, and high worth to the Shof and the Witanayemot. She had suggested that he be given a patent of nobility.

She would do the same for any man, no matter how base-born, he thought, who had saved her twice from the life of a slave-whore. Her gratitude went that far but no further, and she certainly was not in love with him.

He hurled himself into the labors of creating airplanes. Day and night, he worked. In addition to the airplane factory and organizing the Blodland Shoflich Lyftwaepon (Blodland Royal Air Force), he designed a carbine and a tank for the ground forces. He also spent some time in trying to educate the military medical branch in cleanliness and treatment of wounds. After a short and fierce struggle, he had to give up. This world had no Pasteur as yet, and it was not about to accept Two Hawks as one. In the meantime, soldiers would die unnecessarily of infections, typhoid and smallpox, and women would die of puerperal fever. Two Hawks cursed the forces of darkness and prejudice and went back furiously to the business of building better tools for killing.

A month after he had arrived at Bammu, the Perkunishans invaded the island. The Perkunishan and New Cretan fleets slugged it out with the Blodlandish navy in the Narwe Lagu. The defenders inflicted heavy damage and made the enemy pay with two ships for every one of their own. But it lost two-thirds of its own strength, including all but two dreadnoughts, and had to run for it. The Blodlandish air fleet had engaged the Perkunishan at the same time as the surface battle. It was a disaster for both sides; it ended in a draw with exactly forty airships on both sides going down in flames.

Nature seemed to be allied with the invaders. The channel was unnaturally smooth and the winds were slight the day the enemy landed. For five days, the weather conditions held. At the end of that time, the enemy had established a beach-head five miles wide and five miles deep. To accomplish this, they had sacrificed 20,000 men.

A New Cretan army landed on the southern Irish shore and advanced rapidly, again with disproportionate casualties.

Then, winter struck. It was such a winter as Two Hawks had never known. Within a month, the two islands were covered with great drifts of snow. The arctic winds howled down from the north; the temperature dropped to 30 below. Two Hawks shivered and dressed in polar bear furs. Yet this was only the beginning. Before winter was finished with its icy rage, the thermometer would be the equivalent of minus 40 degrees fahrenheit.

He thought that surely the fighting would stop now. Nobody could carry on efficiently—if at all—in this frozen hell. But the invaded and invader alike were used to the severity. They fought on, and where armored cars and trucks bogged down, men on skis or snowshoes pulled toboggans of supplies. Men fell and were buried in the snow. Mile by bloody mile, the Perkunishans claimed Blodlandish territory, and near winter's end were holding the white lands which corresponded to the Kent, Sussex, Surrey, and Hampshire of Earth 1's England.

By then, Two Hawks had twenty monoplanes, all armed with machine guns and with skis for landing gear. He had trained four young men to fly, although in this cold it was difficult even to get the motors to start. The four then became instructors. By the spring thaw, the Lyftwaepn had a hundred fighter planes, a hundred and fifty pilots, and two hundred students.

Espionage informed Two Hawks that Raske had five hundred first-line craft and 800 qualified pilots.

It was then that he got the idea for his self-propelled icesleds. Why not build a vehicle that moved on runners and was propelled by an airplane motor? A fleet of such could operate on the frozen surface of the straits and channel. It could cut up the lines supplying materiel to the invading forces. If enough supplies could be destroyed, the Perkunishans on the island would find themselves short of food and ammunition when the spring thaw came. The waters between mainland and island would be unnavigable at that time. Before the waters were fit for renewal of supply, a big push by the Blodlandish could destroy the food-short, ammunition short, personnel-short enemy.

His suggestion was rejected. The High Command thought the idea was too radical. Two Hawks told the Command he did not understand their pig-headed blindness. His only answer was a savage lecture on keeping his place. Old Lord Raedaesh, a stiff old man with bushy white whiskers and eye pale and cold as sea-ice, delivered the lecture. Raedaesh had made it plain from the start that he regarded Two Hawks as an upstart who was not quite sane. He had opposed the use of the newfangled flying machines for anything other than observation purposes. If it had not been for the orders of the Shof, Raedaesh would never had permitted this wasting of men and materials for such nonsense.

Two Hawks listened until he could control himself no more. Interrupting Lord Raedaesh, he pleaded with the others to listen to him. The iceboats could do more than cut off the enemy supply lines. They could destroy the entire Perkunishan navy. The ships were all in icelocked harbors, and the Blodlandish knew where each was. A fleet of iceboats could cross the ice, even into the North Sea and Baltic, and could torpedo every immobile dreadnaught and cruiser, destroyer, troop ship, supply ship.

Now was the time to act, this day, before the spring thaw started. The propellers and motors of his planes could be mounted on the iceboats. These would carry a crew, machine guns, torpedoes, even small cannon. Iceboats to carry commando troops could be built. If the idea sounded fantastic, a desperate situation demanded desperate action.

Lord Raedaesh, his face scarlet, thundered at him to get out of the council room. He was to get back to his flying toys and his unsportsmanlike rapid-fire weapons. Let him not dare to annoy the High Command any more with his madman schemes.

Trembling, inwardly raging, Two Hawks obeyed. He could do nothing else. Returning to his house, he told Kwasind, "I'll adopt a what-the-hell attitude. Laugh at Raedaesh and his fellow asses. After all, they're just being human, that is, living fossils, stupid tradition-shelled turtles. They are no different from their counterparts on my Earth, past and present. Kwasind, I could tell you the history of man's stupidity on Earth, especially the stupidity of the typical military mind. You'd be shocked."

"The Blodlandish don't have a monopoly on stupidity, arrogance, or rigidity," Kwasind said. "Have you heard the latest?"

New Crete and Perkunisha were at war. The New Cretan forces in Ireland had depended largely upon their ally to supply them during the winter. But the Perkunishans had been very tight-fisted with the supplies. They gave the excuse that they were having enough trouble providing for their own troops. The Shofet of New Crete had seen the real reason behind his ally's actions. Although Perkunisha had pledged Ireland as a prize of war, it wanted the island for itself. If the New Cretans were defeated and Perkunisha had to take over, Perkunisha could claim Ireland by right of conquest.

The Shofet had accused his ally of betrayal. The arrogant Perkunishans reacted violently and swiftly. Even now their Mediterranean fleet and troops in south Rasna were fighting their former allies.

"They think they can take on the whole world," Kwasind said. "Now, they go too far—I hope. That's not all, you know. Perkunisha has demanded that Ikhwan hand back the African colonies it's occupied. And it's also told Ikhwan to stay out of western Dravidia. If Ikhwan doesn't obey, Perkunisha will declare war on them."

"What's the Blodlandish government doing about this? Ikhwan has a powerful navy, probably the most powerful, now that the Perkunisha had lost so many ships. If the Ikhwan would become allied to us . . ."

"They won't. Obviously, they plan to let Europe tear itself apart. Then they'll move in. You watch."

"It's Fimbulwinter," Two Hawks said. "Gotterdammerung. The Twilight of the Gods."

But the winter passed without the end of the world. The snows melted; mud had its fun with the armies that tried to slog through it. The Blodlandish were well entrenched in strategic positions, their cannons in place. The Perkunishans had to haul their big artillery wherever they were needed. Since the few paved roads on the island had been blown up by the retreating Blodlandish, the invaders had to build new ones. This took time, and their armies bogged down.

The Blodlandish Air Force had its first big engagement with the enemy planes, 20 miles south of Bammu. Although outnumbered by ten craft, the Blodlandish fought fiercely. They lost six planes and sent twelve enemy down in flames. Two Hawks was flying that day because he believed his men needed an experienced combat man with them.

The fliers, based on the northern side of the capital city, flew ten sorties that day. Two Hawks went up a second time, leading fifty planes in an attack on the enemy field closest to the front lines. The twenty planes on the ground, all hangars, a bomb dump, and four anti-aircraft posts were destroyed. For two weeks, the Blodlandish flew from dusk to dawn. They lost heavily in the many dogfights over Bammu, since the

Perkunishans were intent on destroying the islanders' air effectiveness. Fortunately, the full weight of their enemy's air arm was not brought to bear against them. Espionage said that Raske had wanted to use every plane he had in the campaign, but the High Command had vetoed this. Half went to fight against the New Cretans; only a fourth were being used on the island.

Raske was in Berlin, probably afraid to leave it because of politics. He had many enemies among the nobility, who would take advantage of his absence to dislodge him if they could. The commander of the Perkunishan Air Force in Blodland was an ex-dirigible man who had not even learned to fly heavier-than-air craft. He did not understand the effective use of his craft. The officers who led their men into aerial combat were as inexperienced as those they led. Since the flight leader's planes were always marked with a scarlet plumed helmet, they got a concentrated attack from the Blodlandish. Two Hawks had given the orders that the flight commanders should be dealt with first, if possible. It became almost certain death for a commander to engage in combat, yet, if he did not, he would have been regarded as a coward by the men under him. The rate of promotion in the invading air force became rapid.

This was very satisfying to Two Hawks, but his successes seemed to have little effect upon the battling on the ground. The enemy took one fort after another, one town after another, losing three-to-one in the process but seemingly not caring. Suddenly, the capital was invaded. A fleet bombarded the forts at the mouth of the Tems river for a week, then landed troops. The Perkunishan air force provided a cover that day. Two Hawks led his complete force against them, and in one day the Perkunishans fliers were almost wiped out.

It made no difference to the men on the ground. In seven days, the invaders were hammering at the gates of Bammu.

Two days later, fifty of Raske's new twin-engined bombers landed on a Perkunishan field. They refueled and took off to bomb Bammu, escorted by a hundred new fighter planes. Only half the bombers returned and 60 fighters. Two Hawks shot down ten enemy that day, bringing his score up to fifty-one. He returned with only thirty Blodlandish, all that remained of his pilots.

15

DESPITE THE staggering losses, the bombing raid was a success. Four bombs struck the Witenayemot while the lords were in final session, before evacuating to the north. Old Lord Raedaesh was killed. Two Hawks thought that this was the best thing that could happen for the Blodlandish. But the bomb had also killed the Shofet, his two younger brothers, the queen, and the Shofet's children. The entire royal family was wiped out, except for the Shofet's uncle, who had been in a madhouse for twenty years. In the confusion that followed the announcement of the disaster, a young Kreion (General) named Erik Leonitha, a bastard son of the mad uncle, declared himself the protector of Blodland. He ordered the army out of Bammu to take a position to the north. He freed the slaves in a proclamation that declared that slavery was at an end forever in Blodland. This was not done out of democratic principle but to keep the slaves from revolting. The Perkunishan agents had been spreading disaffection among them since before the war.

Erik Leonitha also promised that after the enemy had been driven out, more rights would be given the common people and they would have a chance to advance themselves in the military and in the big businesses. The nobility were strongly opposed to him, so he needed as much support as he could get from the masses.

Two Hawks, acting on his own, had given orders to dismantle the aircraft factory and move the machinery to the north. He stayed in Bammu until the last piece of equipment had been loaded on a freight train. He and Kwasind boarded the final train out of the city. Even as he stepped onto his car, shells burst not more than a quarter-mile away. He went through several cars crowded with officers and high-born refugees. While going through an aisle, he heard his name

140

called. He turned to look down into the blue eyes of Ilmika Thorrsstein.

"It's been a long time, Milady," he said. "I heard about your mother and brothers. I sent a letter of condolence. Did you get it?"

"No," she said. "The mails are so bad now. But I thank you for your sympathy."

He tried to continue the conversation without much success. She seemed withdrawn. Perhaps, he thought, she was just too tired. Her face was pale, and she had large dark circles under her eyes. He excused himself, saying he hoped to be able to talk with her again before they reached their destination. After passing through two more jammed aisles, he found his compartment. It was a tiny room, but he was fortunate to get it. The army had reserved it for him and for another important man, a Kreion. The officer rose when Two Hawks entered and returned the salute. Then, to Two Hawks' surprise, he held out his hand to be shaken.

"I am Lord Humphrey Gilbert," he said. "The fates have been good to me. I've been wanting to meet you for a long time."

Two Hawks looked curiously at him. Gilbert was a name of French origin, or so he had always believed until now. There was neither a French nation nor language in this world, so he must have been mistaken. Yet he felt a warmth at coming across something that reminded him of his lost world, coincidence or not.

Gilbert was a short and husky man, about fifty. His thick greying hair was curly, and he had thick black eyebrows, grey eyes, a broad face, and a double chin. His moustache was dark and long and pointed. Gilbert invited Two Hawks to sit down, which Two Hawks would have done anyway, since he had no intention of standing. Gilbert began to talk to Two Hawks as if he had known him a long time. Two Hawks warmed up to him even more, since most of the aristocracy he had met had treated him somewhat coldly or over-politely. As it turned out, Gilbert had, in a way, known Two Hawks for a long time. He had been learning as much as he could about him.

"I inherited my title from my father," Gilbert said. "He came from a middle-class but very wealthy merchant family, most of whose riches came from a large fleet of merchant ships. Now, I have lost all my lands, most of my ships, well, this is not relevant to my story, except that I want you to know my background. You see, my family was founded by my great-great-great, I forget how many greats, grandfather. He came to Blodland in the Year of Hemilka 560."

Two Hawks calculated the date, comparing it to the equivalent date of Earth 1. Hemilka 560 would be 1583 A.D.

"My ancestor, also named Humphrey Gilbert, did not come from the mainland. He came out of the western ocean, the Okeanos, in a ship such as no man had ever seen before."

Gilbert paused as if waiting for a reaction of some sort. Two Hawks looked blank. Gilbert continued, "The ship was *The Squirrel*, sister ship to *The Golden Hind*."

Gilbert looked disappointed when Two Hawks merely looked politely interested. He said, "It's apparent to me that the disappearance of my ancestor from your world made no more than a ripple in your history, if that. I had thought he might have been a man of note. Well, no matter. Humphrey Gilbert was an Englishman—ah, I see your eyes light up now! He was one of the early sailors to the continent of America . . ."

"How do you know all this, I mean, about Englishmen and America?" Two Hawks said.

Gilbert raised a fat hand. "Patience! I'll get to that presently. As I was saying, his ship had been in a storm which separated it from its sister ship. When the storm disappeared, Gilbert could not locate the other ship, so he sailed on back until he came to what he thought was England and home. He sailed into the port of Ent (Earth 1's Bristol). There he and his men were regarded as madmen. But to Gilbert and his crew, the others were mad. What had happened? Here was a people who looked something like the English but were speaking a tongue that only distantly resembled it. Nothing that they had known was familiar. Where were they?

"The Blodlandish locked up the whole crew in an insane asylum. Some of the sailors did go insane, but my ancestor must have been a very adaptable man. He finally convinced the authorities he was harmless. After he was released, he became a sailor and eventually a captain of a ship. He went into African slave-trading—Africa was just being opened up then—and became wealthy. He married well and died rich and highly respected.

"He was intelligent enough not to insist on the truth of the story he had told when he'd first sailed into Ent. In fact, he never again mentioned it. But he did write down his story, plus a history of his native world. He titled it *An Unpublished Romance, or Through the Ivory Gates of the Sea*. The manuscript has been in the family library since his death. Most of his descendants have not read it, and those who did thought their ancestor had a rather feverish imagination."

Gilbert paused, then said, "I never thought so. There were too many consistent details in his history. He had tried to put down the whole of his world on paper. He even wrote an English-Blodlandish comparative grammar and dictionary. I became fascinated by the manuscript—which has more than 5,000 pages—and made the study of it my hobby. I investigated the tales of other strange appearances and became convinced that another Erthe existed. And that, from time to time, men somehow passed from one world to another.

"Are you sure you've never heard of Sir Humphrey Gilbert?"

Two Hawks shook his head. "If I read anything about him, I've forgotten it. And I'm an omnivorous reader, too. I graze in all fields."

"Perhaps he was only one of many who perished during their explorations. It doesn't matter. What does is that your presence here verifies his story. It is more than a fantasy. And my research has convinced me of one thing. The 'gates' are certain weak spots in the forces that separate the two universes. They only open at infrequent intervals, perhaps most of them never more than once."

He leaned towards Two Hawks, his eyes bright. "But I believe that I've located one gate that is more or less permanent. At least, it is in one place, and it has opened up more than once and may again."

Two Hawks became excited. "You know of such a place? Where?"

"I've never actually seen it," Gilbert replied. "I was planning to take a trip there to investigate, but the war stopped me. However, I came across a reference to something that sounds like a gate while I was reading a book on the sorcerers of Hivika."

Hivika, Two Hawks thought. That was the name of the chain of islands that was the only prominent feature of the sunken North American continent. He had seen their name on maps. From their location, they should be the upper part

of the Rockies. The largest island was approximately where
the state of Colorado was on Earth 1.

Polynesians, immigrants from Hawaii, inhabited the
mountainous islands. And, so far, Hivika had remained neutral and independent. The Hivikan inhabitants, like the Maori
of Earth 1, had learned early how to make guns and gun-
powder on their own and how to use them effectively. The
first Old Worlders to make contact with the Hivikans had
not been Europeans but the Arabic Ikhwani of South Africa.
These had carried on trade with Hivika for a hundred years
before the first Blodlandish ship had accidentally discovered
the islands. The Europeans found a handsome and intelligent
brown people who mined iron and gold, sailed ships armed
with cannon, and were not awed by the white man's technology. Moreover, the Hivikans had gone through several plagues
brought to them by the Ikhwan. The descendants of the survivors were fairly resistant to European diseases.

Gilbert said, "The Hivika still practice the old religion,
you know. Their priests, who claim to be sorcerers, keep
constant vigilance over certain tabu places. One of these is a
cave high up on the loftiest mountain of the largest island.
Not much is known about the cave, but a Perkunishan scholar
found out some things. The priests call the cave The Hole
Between The Worlds. Terrible sounds sometimes come
from the rear of the cave, where the Hole sometimes appears.
The back wall of the cave seems to dissolve, and the priests
get glimpses into another world. Perhaps *world* is not the
right translation for the word they use. It could mean the Place
of the Gods. The priests dare not go near the 'gate,' because
they believe that the chief god, Ke Aku'a, lives in this world."

Two Hawks said, "This is too good to be true. I'm afraid
to get too excited about it. It'll probably turn out to be
some natural phenomenon."

"The gates are natural phenomena," Gilbert said. "It's
certainly worth investigating, don't you agree?"

"I intend to investigate," Two Hawks said. "In fact, I'd
like to leave for Hivika right now. Only, it's impossible."

"When the war's over, we might go together. If there is
a gate through which we could pass, I'd like very much to see
the Earth of my ancestor."

Two Hawks did not reply, but he was thinking that, for
Gilbert, Earth 1 might be an interesting place to visit but
not to live in. Gilbert would have the same sense of disloca-

tion, of utter severance, that Two Hawks and O'Brien had had. Even now, despite an increasing familiarity with this planet, Two Hawks never felt quite at ease. He just did not *belong*.

However, it was a feeling he could endure with no more than a little bit of discomfort and out-of-jointedness most of the time. The nights were the worse, when he was alone.

Somebody knocked on the compartment door. Two Hawks opened it, a young officer saluted and said, "Beg your pardon, Koiran. The Lady Thorrsstein has taken ill, and she's asked for you."

Two Hawks followed the officer into Ilmika's car. He found her lying on the seat, surrounded by solicitous men. She was very pale but had recovered from her faint. A doctor standing over her said to Two Hawks, "She'll be all right as soon as she gets something to eat."

Two Hawks said, "Ilmika, why didn't you ask. . . ?" He stopped, then said, "No, you'd be too proud."

"Hers is not an uncommon story in these unhappy times," the doctor said. "There are many high-born who have lost their lands—money, everything but their titles. And . . ."

The doctor closed his mouth as if he had said too much. Two Hawks looked sharply at him. He seemed to be deriving some sort of satisfaction from Ilmika's condition. Probably, he was a commoner, and, like many, shared the repressed but very keen resentment of the lower classes towards the privileged. Two Hawks understood their feeling, since the majority suffered hardships and injustices exceeding those of the lower classes of the early 18th century of his own planet. Nevertheless, he was angry at the doctor. Ilmika was a human being who had also gone through many privations and griefs. Her family was dead; her home and possessions were in the hands of the enemy. And, as he talked to her while he fed her hot soup, he discovered she did not have a coin to her name.

She wept while she drank the soup. "I couldn't help fainting. Now, everybody knows how destitute I am. I am a charity case. The name of Thorrsstein is disgraced."

"Disgraced?" he said quietly. "If you are, so is three-fourths of the nobility of Blodland. Why should you be so proud? It's the fault of the war, not you. Besides, now is the time to show that nobility is made of stronger stuff than a mere name. You have to act noble to be noble."

She smiled weakly. He got a slice of ham from one officer and a piece of bread from another and fed them to her. When she had finished eating, she whispered to him, "If only I could get away from their stares."

"There's room in my compartment for you," he said. He lifted her up, and, supporting her, got her to his compartment. She lay down on one of the seats and was quickly asleep. When she awoke late that evening, he had supper with her in the compartment. Gilbert had gone to the dining car, and Kwasind was outside the door, so they were alone. Two Hawks waited until they had eaten the cold and coarse food. Then he asked her if she would work for him. He needed a secretary, he said. She turned so red that he thought he had angered her. But when he heard her stammer, he understood that she had mistaken the intent of the offer.

He laughed, although he was not amused, and said, "No, Milady, I am not asking you to be my mistress. You will have to do nothing beyond the requirements of your secretarial duties."

She said, "Why shouldn't I be your whore? I owe you so much."

"You don't owe me that much! Even if you did, I'd never ask you to pay up. I want a woman who loves me—or at least desires me.

She was still red in the face, but she looked steadily into his eyes.

"If I did not desire you, do you think I'd accept your food and lodging now? Do you think me so empty of pride?"

He stood up and then leaned over her. She raised her face and closed her eyes for his kiss. Her arms came up around his neck, and she rose. She worked her mouth against his and pressed her body against him.

He pushed her away. "You're trying too hard. You don't really want to kiss me."

"I'm sorry," she said. Turning away, she began to weep. "Does no one want me? Do you reject me because I have been dishonored by those beasts in Itskapintik?"

Two Hawks turned her to face him. He said, "Ilmika, I don't understand you. Are you doing this because you feel that your virtue was taken away by an act of force?"

"Don't you know? There's not a nobleman in Blodland who'd have me now, since my story is known."

"So you'll take me because I'm a commoner, and commoners

don't care about virtue in their women? Or a commoner should be delirious with joy to get a noblewoman, no matter what her state of virtue? I'm the last refuge, right?"

She slapped him hard. Then she came at him with her fingernails. He caught her wrists and held her away from him.

"You dumb bitch! I love you! I don't give a damn about your virginity! I love you and want you to love me! But I'll be go-to-hell if I'll have a woman who thinks of me as being so low I can't refuse even her! You're not going to punish yourself by punishing me!"

He shoved her so hard she fell on the seat, and he said, "The offer is still good. Give me your decision when we reach Tolkinham. Meanwhile, I'm getting out."

He slammed the door behind him. The rest of the night, he slept sitting on the floor of the aisle, propped against the side of a seat. He did not sleep well. When the train pulled into Tolkinham, he returned to the compartment. Gilbert was the only one in it.

"Where did Thorrsstein go?" Two Hawks said.

"I don't know. I thought she went to say goodbye to you."

Two Hawks pushed through the crowd on the aisle, drawing some black looks and muttered rebukes. Once outside, he looked through the station. She was gone. He thought of sending Kwasind to look for her, but an officer stopped him. He was handed his latest orders, which were to report to the Kreion Grettirsson. Two Hawks wondered why an infantry general wanted him. He hitchhiked a ride on an army car to the big camp outside Tolkinham and went to the Kreion's camp. Grettirsson informed him that the Blodlandish Lyftwaepn was no more. The shortage of gas and oil was so acute that fuel supplies would be reserved for military ground vehicles only. Two Hawks was to serve as commander of a regiment of armored cars. That is, he would until the gas ran completely out. Then he would be an infantryman.

Two Hawks left the tent knowing that the island was doomed. Within a month or two, the Perkunishans would own Blodland.

During the four weeks of fighting that followed, Two Hawks heard about developments in Perkunisha. Despite triumphs abroad, all had not gone well in Berlin. The two sons of the Kassandras had been killed in a train wreck. The Blodlandish agents reported their doubts about the wreck being an accident. On hearing of his sons' deaths, the Kassandras was paralyzed by a stroke. Six days later, he died of pneumonia. His male heir, a nephew, was assassinated on his way to Berlin. The Perkunishans accused Blodland of the killing and soon after accused it of having caused the train wreck. Blodland denied any connection with the deaths. The Blodlandish agents had their own suspicions, all of which pointed at Raske.

The German's ambitions were well known. He wanted to marry the Kassandras' daughter. If he did, he would become Prince Consort—provided that the Grand Council made her queen. The Council was convening now, debating whether to crown her or to choose a Kassandras from a list of male nobles.

Meanwhile, the armies in the field conducted business as usual. The Protector of Blodland, Erik Leonitha, proved to be a brilliant tactician. Three times he defeated the invaders in large-scale battles. Each time, he had to retreat, unable to hold the ground he had won. The Perkunishans brought up new armies, strong with fresh troops and superior weapons. The enemy air force, no longer having Two Hawks' planes to fear, made northern Blodland hideous with strafing and bombing attacks.

Then, the Blodlandish fuel supply was gone. The army retreated on foot to their last stand. The enemy planes harassed them, and the enemy armor bit at their heels. Two Hawks and Kwasind, riflemen now, made it to Ulfstal. Two Hawks was handed a note from Humphrey Gilbert. He read it, then said, "Kwasind, Ilmika is a nurse in the army hospital here. And before that she was working in an ammunition factory. She has guts. I knew I wasn't in love with just a pretty face."

Kwasind was not tactful. "She may have guts. But does she love you?"

"I don't know. I'm still hoping. Maybe she's supporting herself just to show me she can be independent. Maybe she'll come to me as an equal after she's proved she doesn't have to take me because I'm the only one who'll have her."

"A woman is not the equal of a man," Kwasind said. "You should have taken her and taught her to love you. What is all this talk about independence? A woman should be dependent upon a man."

Two Hawks went looking for Ilmika that evening. He

found the hospital, but it had been bombed and was no longer used. The wounded were in tents around the gutted building. It took him an hour to locate her in a large tent on the edge of the camp.

Seeing him enter, she was so startled she dropped a roll of bandages. She picked the roll up off the dirt floor, evidently intending to use it without sterilizing it. He said nothing about the bandages, since he had long ago learned that it was useless to protest. These people knew nothing of germs and did not want to hear about them.

"Greetings, my lord," she said.

"Health to you, Milady. Dammit, Ilmika, don't be so formal! We've been through too much for this my-lord-my-lady crap!"

She smiled and said, "You are right—as usual. What are you doing here?"

"I could say I came to visit with a sick friend."

"Do you mean me?"

He nodded and said, "Will you marry me?"

She gasped and almost dropped the bandages again.

"Surely, you're . . . You shouldn't joke about a thing like that."

He put his hands on her shoulders and said, "Why should I be joking? You know I love you. I couldn't ask you to be my wife before because . . . well, you know all the reasons too well. But things have changed. Blueblood, class barriers don't mean much any more. And if Blodland wins or loses the war, things will never be the same again. And if you can ever quit thinking like an aristocrat, look at me as a woman looks at a man, we can be happy.

"Can you do that?"

She did not reply. He waited until he could stand the silence no more.

"Say yes or say no!"

"Yes!"

He took her in his arms and kissed her. She did not seem to be trying to imitate passion this time.

A doctor interrupted them and ordered her to get back to work. Two Hawks said, "Ilmika, if things go badly tomorrow, I'll try to meet you in Lefswik. I'll be shipping out to Dublin from there if we're defeated here—and I expect we will be. I have plans for us, but there's no time to talk about them. Meanwhile, I love you!"

Tears in her eyes, she whispered, "I love you. But, Roger, I'm afraid of tomorrow. What if I don't ever see you again?"

"Then you won't. But it'll only be because I'll be dead."

She shivered.

"Don't say that!"

"Everything should be said."

He gave her a final kiss and walked away, returning the doctor's glare with a smile. On the way back to his quarters, he was stopped by a noncom, who told him he was to report to the Protector. Wondering what Leonitha wanted of him, Two Hawks followed the noncom to the pavilion-tent. He had to identify himself to two officer-guards before he was admitted. This security precaution was necessary, since assassination of high-ranking officers was normal procedure in war. In fact, the Protector had narrowly escaped being killed two days before. One of the unsuccessful Perkunishans had shot himself in the head before he could be taken. The other was too seriously wounded to kill himself. When he regained consciousness, he was hung upside down over a bonfire.

16

IN THE TENT, Two Hawks snapped to a salute before the Protector, seated behind a desk. His arm, however, did not fall back to his hip with the prescribed swiftness. Two Hawks was too astounded at sight of the man on a chair at the rear of the tent.

"Raske!"

The German grinned and waved airily.

"My old friend—and enemy—the red-skinned Two Hawks!" he said.

A beautiful blonde woman sat on another chair by Raske. She was richly dressed, and her neck, fingers, and arms glittered with gems. Two Hawks guessed at once that she was Persinai, daughter of the Kassandras.

The Protector explained their presence. A new Kassandras has been elected by the Grand Council. One of his first acts had been to order the arrest of Raske. The German was charged with the assassination of the heirs to the throne.

Raske had been one step ahead of him. He had talked the Kassandras' daughter into running away with him. The two fled from Perkunisha in one of the new two-engined fighter planes. Raske landed at a field in Rasna (Earth 1's France) and brazened his way through. He got his plane refueled, after which he got as far as a meadow on the eastern coast of northern England.

He and his bride were asking for sanctuary.

"I don't know whether I should shoot him or listen to him," the Protector said. "He's worth nothing as a hostage, and it's too late to use his technical knowledge."

Raske said, "If you can scrape up enough gas, I'll fly Two Hawks to Ireland. Blodland will need both of us, since you will have to make a last stand there."

Two Hawks said, "Ireland doesn't have any gas, either. So what good could we do there?"

"I'll tell you something the Perkunishans have been keeping very secret. There won't be any invasion of Ireland until next year. Perkunisha has overextended itself. It's committed so deeply on the mainland and here that it can't launch another major campaign. Of course, Perkunisha will try to bluff. It'll demand that the Blodlandish forces in Ireland unconditionally surrender. But if you refuse, if you hold out, you'll have a year to make preparations. By then, you may have supplies, gas, oil, ammunition. I've been in touch with the Ikhwani. They're willing to provide all Ireland needs. And they've no fear of the Perkunishan navy. They figure it's been too weakened by its losses."

Raske started to rise but was restrained by the guard behind him.

"If Two Hawks and I will give the Ikhwani all the information they need to build an air force, they'll aid Blodland!"

The Protector spoke to Two Hawks. "Can we believe him?"

"Oh, yes, you can. I don't doubt that he's been dealing with Ikhwan, just in case he did have to run for his life. But all this about Ikhwan rearming and resupplying us in Ireland is hogwash. Even if the Ikhwan dared to run battleships and freight ships to Ireland, they'd be blasted out of the waters. The Perkunishan air force would take care of that. No, there's no hope from Ikhwan."

"I thought so," the Protector said. He spoke to Raske, "You're going to the guardhouse while I decide what to do with you. Your wife will be lodged in a house, where she'll be treated well. After all, she's the Kassandras' daughter. What happens to you, Raske, depends upon the outcome of the battle tomorrow. If we lose, Perkunisha will have you, and I suppose you'll be shot on sight. If we win . . . well, I may shoot you. Because of you and your flying machines, Blodland is denied a chance to arm itself again in Ireland."

As Raske was escorted from the tent, Two Hawks said, "Tough luck, my kraut friend. You lived high on the hog for a while, higher than you ever would have on Earth 1. Be content with that."

Raske grinned back at him. "Red-skin, I'm not dead yet. I'll see you later, that is, if you're alive."

Two Hawks watched him being marched off and thought that Raske's words were more than bravado. Tomorrow's battle might be Two Hawk's last. As it turned out, it was almost—but not quite. Four times during the day, he was slightly wounded by shell fragments, by grenade fragments, and once by a bayonet during hand-to-hand combat. Dusk came, and with it the Blodlandish retreated northward. Two Hawks and Kwasind walked west, since they thought that the main part of the Perkunishan army would be streaming upland, hot for the kill.

"We could take to the hills and lead a miserable life as guerrilla fighters," Two Hawks told Kwasind. "Eventually, if we didn't starve, we'd get caught. So, it's to the coast for us and a boat to Ireland. What the hell, we don't owe these people anything! It's not our fight; it's not even my world. I'm getting to Hivika—somehow."

They arrived at the port of Lefswik on the edge of the Irish Sea. Lefswik was crowded with refugees, all wanting to take passage on the four large steamers and the score of smaller ones. Two Hawks did not have much hope of being allowed on board unless he could find some important official to secure a berth for him. He had, however, not even gotten to the docks before he heard his name called. He turned to see the fat body of Humphrey Gilbert pushing through the crowds. Gilbert was smiling and waving a handful of papers.

"Two Hawks! My fellow Earthman! What luck! I've been looking for you, hoping that you'd show up, despite all the odds against your doing so! I can get you into my stateroom! You'll have to sleep on the floor! But hurry! The ship leaves in thirty-five minutes! I'd just about given up all hope!"

"Did you see Ilmika Thorrsstein?" Two Hawks said.

"Did I see her?" the fat man jumped up and down in glee. "She's in my stateroom, too! She . . . never mind . . . she came looking for you, and she's all right! Lovers reunited, joy requited, and all that!"

Two Hawks was too happy to reply. He heard only half of Gilbert's chatter. They were stopped at the bottom of the gangplank where an official took an exasperating amount of time going over the papers. He did not, however, give them an argument. If he had, he would have found himself thrown into the water by Kwasind's huge hands. Two Hawks would have stormed the ship to get to Ilmika, a foolish move, since the marines at the upper end of the gangway would have shot him down.

He was not so caught up with his rapture, however, that he did not see a familiar face in the mob on the foredeck. He stopped, looked again, and then shook his head. It could not be.

But he was not mistaken. Blond, curly-headed, handsome Raske was grinning at him. The German waved his hand and then turned and disappeared into the crowd. His feeling that he would not be betrayed by Two Hawks was correct. Two Hawks wondered how Raske had gotten out of the guardhouse and made his way here and on board a vessel which was taking only the elite of the refugees. He would find out later. Meantime, if Raske was clever and quick enough to make good his escape, he could have it. For the time being, anyway. All Two Hawks wanted now was to hold Ilmika in his arms.

This he did, although with no privacy. Besides Gilbert and Kwasind, there were five others in the cabin. They pretended to ignore the two lovers and talked on as if nothing were happening. Looking up momentarily from between kisses, Two Hawks saw them glancing covertly at him, their amusement or embarrassment apparent. He did not care.

The ship left the harbor and gained speed as swiftly as its laboring engines would allow. It was not safe now nor would it be even after it docked in Dublin. At any moment, Perkunishan planes could appear to strafe and bomb. Then, a fog set in, and they were secure—provided they did not ram another ship or run afoul of reefs close to the Irish shore.

Two Hawks hated to do it, yet he had to find Raske and determine what he was up to. He still was not sure that he would not turn the German in. Raske represented no genuine threat to the Blodlandish at the moment. He could do little against them or for them, although he might possibly be very valuable later on. Or he might end up being a Blodlandish nobleman or even their ruler. Two Hawks would put nothing past Raske.

He found him sitting on a blanket on the deck. There were others close but half-hidden by the thick fog. Two Hawks called his name until the German answered. Two Hawks said, "Where's Persinai?"

"She's dead," Raske said unemotionally. "Right after we escaped—and I must tell you about that some time, my redskinned friend, you wouldn't believe how I got out . . . well, I had weapons; I gave her a gun. And she killed herself. She'd been despondent ever since she was put in the guardhouse; conscience, I think. She felt guilty because she'd deserted her people. And she blamed me for her father's death, hence herself, for having fallen in love with me."

Two Hawks was silent for a while. Raske's story could be true. On the other hand, he was capable of abandoning her if he thought she would hinder him. Whatever the truth, it would probably never be known by any but Raske.

"What do you think the future holds for us—for us two Earthmen?" Raske said. "We might be safe in Ireland for a while. I know that Perkunisha doesn't intend to invade it until next year, maybe not for two years, if Ireland gives no trouble. Perkunisha is overextended as it is; it wants no new wars."

"If—when—Perkunisha finds out we're in Ireland, it'll demand we be turned over to it." Two Hawks said. "You know as well as I do that they won't want us floating around. They think we're too dangerous to them. Which is a laugh."

"What do you mean?" Raske said. His hurt pride showed in his voice.

"This world has already sucked us dry of our—admit it—limited knowledge. We really have nothing more than some technical assistance to give it. It's true the Blodlandish have rejected what I told them about the origin of disease. But they'll come around to it in time. They would have done so in a few years anyway, when some native Pasteur stood up to their superstitions and fought them down. Just as all we have told them would have come about in ten years or less, anyway. We just accelerated science a little bit, that's all."

Raske chuckled. "You know, Two Hawks, you're really right. I was hurt for a minute, but I can recognize the truth when I have to. Only . . . well, I did have what they wanted, and I was parlaying my advantages into an empire for me. If things had gone just a little bit differently."

"They didn't. So here we are. Doomed to be hounded to the ends of the earth because of something we don't have. But try to convince them of that."

He hesitated a moment, then decided not to tell Raske his plans. Raske might be harmless, even useful. However, if he saw a chance to advance himself at Two Hawks' expense, he would not hesitate a moment. He had proven himself capable of murder and, perhaps, even abandoned the woman who had given up her country and title for him. Yet, Two Hawks found it hard not to confide in Raske. There was the tie of Earthkinship between them, and the fellow was so charming. He would smile at you just before putting the knife in, and the strange thing about it was that the smile would ease the pain a little. Or anaesthetize the victim.

Two Hawks thought that, if he could be realistic, he would tell the captain of the ship to throw Raske into the sea

He sighed and rose, saying, "I won't turn you in. But if I hear of any skullduggery on your part, you're done for. And this is goodbye. I don't want to see you anymore, except at a far distance."

"Two Hawks! You hurt me! Why?"

Raske actually did sound as if he had been cut deeply. Two Hawks walked away, knowing that he was possibly letting a wolf loose on this world but unable to sever the bonds of a common universe. Strange as it sounded, Raske's death would be like cutting out part of his own heart.

The rest of the journey was in fog. Dublin was just as mist-shrouded. The passengers disembarked in a wet dusk Gilbert led Ilmika, Two Hawks, and Kwasind to the home of a friend. They were there only one day when news of the plague came.

It was just as it had been thirty years ago, when Perkunisha was on the verge of conquering the Western World. The piles of rotting bodies all over the land, the weakening hunger and deadly winter, the lack of cleanliness, and the thriving of the rats had brought the Black Plague once again.

"Europe is saved from the Perkunishans; God save it now from a far worse fate," Gilbert said. His normally red face was pale, and he was no longer smiling. "My own parents and three of my brothers and two of my sisters died the last time the scourge struck. My aunt brought me to Ireland to escape it, but it followed us, and she, too, died. God help mankind Now you will see such a slaughter as the Perkunishans could envision only in their nightmares. They, too, will die; half of mankind will die in two years."

"If they had listened to me . . ." Two Hawks said. He stopped, shrugged, and resumed. "Do we stay here and die?"

Gilbert said, "No! One of my ships is in port, in fact, the last of my ships. It's provisioned for a long voyage. We'll sail tonight for Hivika! Only, let's hope we get there before Hivika hears of the plague! Otherwise, we'll never be allowed on shore!"

Two Hawks knew what was in his mind besides escaping

ubonic plague. He said, "I'd like to hope, but I don't have much faith in the tales of superstitious witch-doctors."

"Why not?" Gilbert said.

And indeed, why not?

Nevertheless, as the days went by and the Atlantic was the only thing to be seen, the cold gray and sometimes angry ocean, Two Hawks grew less optimistic. Even if there were a 'gate' in a cave on top of that high mountain in Hivika, it probably would not be open. The sorcerers themselves had stated that it only opened every fifty years or so and then only for a few seconds. The last time had been thirty years go. Moreover, there was the problem of gaining access to the cave. Of all the many tabu places on the island, the cave was the most sacred. No one except the few high priests and the king were ever allowed there; the mountain itself, though close to the sea, was walled halfway up its slope and heavily guarded.

Despite his misgivings, Two Hawks enjoyed the trip. He and Ilmika had a chance for a long honeymoon. For the first time, they really became acquainted and found, much to the surprise of both, that they not only loved each other—that is, had a mutual passion—but actually liked each other. They had, of course, certain ways of thought and behavior that aggravated the other. These were both personal and cultural. But they were willing to tell one another when the partner did something to offend, and the friction would be smoothed out. Two Hawks was happy, although he was realistic enough to know that she would always have a certain amount of arrogance. She could not help it, since she had been brought up as an aristocrat in an undemocratic world.

Two Hawks really began to feel uneasy for the first time when the vessel crossed that invisible line which would have been the shore of North America on Earth 1. Almost, he expected the ship to shudder, then rise up out of the water on a slope of land with a great crash and grind. But the *Twaelgold* continued on smoothly while somewhere below was New Foundland. It went over the area in which the city of New York would have been; he imagined a sunken metropolis of skyscrapers and human bones on the streets, over which fish swam. It was sheer fantasy, of course, since in his world no man had ever seen that area. It was at least 5,000 feet below the surface, cold and dark and covered with slimy mud.

There was no part of the North or South Americas above water which had not been, on Earth 1, at six thousand feet above sea level. In the Northern Hemisphere, only a few small islands in the east (the highest part of the Appalachians on Earth 1) and a chain of islands, some rather large, in the west, existed. These were inhabited by Polynesians presumably immigrants who had arrived 750 years ago. The South American chains, bigger in area and longer than the North, were populated by colonizers from, presumably, the island known on Earth 1 as Easter Island.

The main island toward which the *Hwaelgold* was heading was composed of highland which, on Earth 1, would have been the mountainous parts of Colorado. The capital city of Kualono was on the eastern sea coast and was a harbor with great stone temples and palaces and massive granite idols, light airy houses ill-adapted to the cold winters, highways of huge close-fitting stone blocks, and vegetation peculiarly North American. The natives wore few clothes in the summer time and played and swam much like their Hawaiian cousins. In the winter, they wore heavy clothes of spun fabric and feathers. There were also iron mines and smelters and factories now, and automobiles on the roads. Despite the increasing industrialization and trade (mainly with the South African Arabs), the Hivikans lived much as they had in the past: easy-going, laughing, playing, and only vicious in their wars. The last one had taken place some fifty years ago and had made more than enough elbow room in an overpopulated land.

Two Hawks spent much time on the bridge with Gilbert. Ilmika sat on a chair in a corner and knitted; Kwasind stood like a bronze statue of Hercules in one corner. Two Hawks, who had drawn a map from memory of the North America of his native world, indicated the Mississippi River.

"We should be about over it," he said. "Rather, where it would be if it existed here."

At that moment, the captain exclaimed. Two Hawks looked up to see him staring through a pair of binoculars to the north. He picked up a pair given him by Gilbert and searched the same quarter of the sea. There, so low on the horizon it could only be viewed with glasses, was a small cloud. The captain, after studying it for a while, gave orders to increase the speed of the *Hwaelgold*. He explained that the vessel might be peaceful, perhaps a merchantman from South Africa,

But if the contact with the ship could be avoided, it would be best.

By dusk, the smoke had come closer. Its estimated speed placed it out of the category of merchant; it could only be a warship, either a destroyer or cruiser. "The direction from which it comes should make it an Ikhwani. But it could be a Perkunishan raider."

At the end of the second day, the pursuer (if it was one) was a little over a mile away. It glittered whitely in the sun and was identifiable as Arabic.

"I don't think they'll sink us," the captain said. "We are too valuable a prize, a large well-built British craft the Ikhwani can use to enrich their merchant fleet. But they can't put a prize crew aboard and take the *Hwaelgold* back to South Africa. It doesn't have enough fuel or provisions to make the voyage. So, the only thing the Arabs can do is to sail us into Kvalono and refuel it there."

"What will happen to us?" Ilmika said.

"The Ikhwani might make some of the sailors help sail the *Hwaelgold* to Ikhwan," he replied. "The rest of us should be left on Hivika, free to make our way back to Blodland as best we can. The Ikhwani won't want to take more prisoners than they can help. After all, they'd have to feed us. Unless we could be used as slaves. That's a possibility. Tell the truth, I don't know. It's up to God and the Ikhwani."

Night fell. The cruiser kept a quarter-mile behind the *Hwaelgold,* its searchlights pinning the merchantman. The captain took no vain evasive action but continued to run his vessel at top speed. He could do nothing else unless the Ikhwani sent a shell over him and ordered him to stop. This the cruiser would undoubtedly do when dawn arrived.

At midnight, the rainstorm that the captain had been praying for swept like a dropped net out of the west. With it came rough seas. Two seconds after the rain and darkness struck, the captain ordered the *Hwaelgold* to turn sharply southwards. In a short time, the lights of the cruiser had disappeared. When the sun came up, it shone only upon the Blodland ship. The captain ordered a normal cruising speed, since he had been worried about his engines giving way under the long strain.

17

THE SEAS WERE EMPTY of alien smoke for the next five days. The dawn of the sixth day, the captain took a reading and verified that their position was only a hundred miles east of Kualono. Within an hour, they should be sighting Miki'ao a small island. Exactly forty minutes later, the 500-foot peak of Miki'ao reared above the horizon. The captains' grin of pride, however, was wiped off when smoke was sighted to the rear. He gave the orders for full speed ahead and spent most of the next two hours watching to the aft. This time, the Ikhwani had approached much closer before being detected. It was coming up fast to the southward and at an angle that would intercept them long before they reached the safety of Kualono.

The captain conferred with Gilbert and then ordered the *Hwaelgold* to turn at a 45-degree angle northward. "There are dangerous reefs just above the harbor," he said. "I know them well. We'll make a run through them; perhaps the Ikhwani will pile up on them. If they don't we'll run it ashore, if there's a place on those forbidding cliffs to do so. In any case, the Arabs won't get their hands on my ship."

Gilbert said, "He's making for Lapu Mountain, where the Cave of the Outer Gods is. If we land there, we'll have good excuse for trespassing on tabu property. We won't get there until a little before dusk. So, if the Hivikans don't see us . . ."

Two Hawks replied to Gilbert's smile with one of his own. "We bulldoze our way in then? Great! And what if the Ikhwani respect the marine sovereignty of Hivika and refuse to follow us in? What do we use for an excuse?"

"If they respected the Hivika sovereignty, they would have quit long ago," the captain said. "Hivika claims extend fifty miles out from the coast. No, they're not going to quit unless they come across a Hivikan naval ship. Maybe not then. Ikhwan would like an excuse to go to war with Hivika; it has coveted Hivika for a long time. Only the threat of war with Blodland and Perkunisha kept them from conquest. Now, I don't know."

The *Hwaelgold*, her engines pounding, beat northwestward. Its pursuer steadily cut down the distance between them. By the time that the black headlands of the coast had become quite high, the cruiser was only a half-mile behind. Then smoke flared out of the muzzle of one of its eight-inchers, and a geyser soared up twenty yards off the starboard bow of the *Hwaelgold*. Twenty seconds later, a second waterspout appeared fifteen yards off the port bow.

By then, the captain was taking his ship on a zigzag course. The path was not chosen at random, however, since the vessel was steering through the narrow channels between the reefs. Some of these were evident only by the darker blue of the water; others were near enough to the surface to cause the seas to boil.

By then, the cruiser had quit firing. Evidently, it had not meant to hit its quarry but had only hoped that the shells would make it surrender. Seeing that the *Hwaelgold* intended to make a run for it, the Ikhwani went after them. It, too, zigged and zagged but at a more cautious pace. Two Hawks wondered why the Arabs were taking such chances. Why should they be so determined to capture them? What was special about the merchantman? Perhaps, their espionage system in Blodland had learned that he was on his way to Hivika. It would then have sent a radio message, by spark-gap transmitter, to an Ikhwani vessel somewhere in the vicinity. And the message would have been relayed by various ships until the cruiser had received it.

This would explain why the *Hwaelgold* had not been sunk. He was wanted alive so that the Arabs could use his knowledge, just as the Perkunishans and Blodlandish had. That would explain not only their hunting through the reefs but their ignoring the Hivika sea-domain.

The mountain of Lapu was at the very edge of the waters. It rose steeply on both the south and north sides; on the eastern, it sloped much more gently and terminated in a wide black-sand beach. Towards this, the captain steered the ship after it had slipped through a narrow channel. There was a slight scraping of the plates of the keel on the rocks, and the vessel was in calmer waters. Captain Wilftik heaved a sigh of relief and grinned.

"The cruiser won't make it through there without tearing her bottom out. I hope she tries it."

He gave orders to stop the ship and to lower two lifeboats. The cruiser did not attempt the passage; it slid on by alongside the reef, turned as closely as it could to avoid another reef, and then pointed her nose outwards. While her engines kept her from drifting backwards against the reef, it lowered two power launches. Two Hawks, observing them through his binoculars, saw that the launches were equipped with several two-inch cannons and mortars. Each held about thirty marines, in addition to the crews. The marines looked like medieval Saracens with their turbans above which rose the gleaming points of the helmets, steel cuirasses, great leather belts, scabbards containing scimitars, scarlet baggy pants, and calf-length boots with turned-up toes. Each had a large blue sack strapped to his belt and carried a rifle.

Captain Wilfrik wanted to run his ship back through the entrance between the reefs and smash the launches just as they came into the passageway on the other end. Gilbert objected. "The cruiser will blow you out of the water. And it will then send another launch with marines after us on land. Hold your fire; permit the landing-party to go after us. The sailors in our party will ambush them, but I'm not asking them to give up their lives for us. They'll do it from a place which the Ikhwani can't take—if they can find one."

Two boats took Two Hawks, Ilmika, Kwasind, Gilbert, and officers and crewmen ashore. They went quickly across the beach and began climbing. The sun had gone down behind the mountain by then, shrouding this side in twilight. Above them and out to the sea, the sky was a bright blue and the waters green. The Ikhwani launches drove their prows onto the sand, and the white and scarlet (twilight-browned) figures were little dolls. The pursued had a twenty-minute headstart and had taken advantage of it. Although they were soon in a dusk so thick it made climbing difficult, they continued. Then the sun plunged down into the sea, and they were slowed even more. They caught hold of bushes and pulled themselves up, occasionally slipping but always able to stop their backward slide by grabbing the vegetation.

Now and then, they came to great gnarled oaks, which Gilbert said had been planted here two hundred years ago by

King Mahimahi. "The mountain above the guard-wall is a thick forest of oaks. We'll be well concealed then—if we can get past the Hivika sentinels."

"I wonder why they haven't spotted us yet?" Two Hawks said. "I know it's dark now, but the guards should have been able to see both ships."

"I don't know," Gilbert replied. "Perhaps they're planning on ambushing us, just as we are the Ikhwani."

Gilbert's fat was telling on him; he was breathing heavily. Aside from his panting, it was quiet on the mountain, with the only sounds being the wind through the oak leaves and the noise of their progress: twigs cracking, wet leaves squishing, a branch springing back with a swishing sound, muffled curses as a man slipped. When they stopped to rest, and Gilbert regained his breath, the silence was like that in a huge cathedral, in the moment when all have bowed their heads and just before the minister launches into a prayer. However, it was no prayer that was to come, Two Hawks felt sure of that. It seemed as if lightning would leap out from the very rubbing of the air against it, or a curse instead of a prayer would crackle down the mountain.

They struggled on up, their path lit only by the stars. Two hours went by, and the moon came out. Three-quarters full, she bounced a bright mercury over the mountain. Thereafter they climbed more surely and more rapidly. The illumination, although advantageous now, would be a danger when they reached the sentinel wall. Two Hawks hoped that the vegetation had not been cleared off between the wall and the oaks and bushes. To venture across a clearing in this brightness was to be revealed at once to any watcher.

Twenty minutes later, they came to the edge of the woods. As he had feared, there was a bare space of forty yards. At its other end, above them at a 50-degree angle, embrasured walls loomed. These were about 20 feet high, composed of huge stone blocks, grey and veined in black, and fitted together without mortar. Every thirty yards along the top of the wall was a slender twenty-foot tower, round and capped with a cone of small mortared rocks.

"Where are the guards?" Gilbert whispered.

The moonlight coated the wall with soft metal; the shiny grey looked as if it would ring at the blow of a hammer. But there was no sound except for the shush-shush of wind through the leaves.

Two Hawks, looking at the dark, narrow, arched entrances on the sides of the towers, said, "If the guards are in there, they're hiding. Well, here goes. Don't anybody follow me until the coast is clear."

With the coil of the rope in his left hand and the three-pronged catching hooks in his right, he ran out from under an oak's shadow. He expected to hear a shout from the black interior of a tower, followed by a tongue of flame and explosion. However, the walls remained as still and shiny grey as before. Reaching the bottom of the ramparts, he paused, gauged the distance to the top, and cast the hooks, the rope uncoiling after them. The hooks sailed through an embrasure just above him and struck with a clank. The noise shocked him. Until that moment he had not realized how unconsciously strong the impression of the *sacredness* of the place had been.

He pulled on the rope, and it became taut as the prongs dug in. Hand over hand, his feet against the wall, almost parallel to the ground, he climbed up. He gripped the lip of the stone and pulled himself up and over and then crouched in the shelf of the embrasure. He waited for an outcry from a guard. When a minute had gone by, he eased himself down into the passageway that ran the length of the wall. It was six feet across and high enough to reach to the top of his head.

He drew his revolver and ran to the stone steps which led up the wall and to the nearest watch tower. Up the steep flight he went and hurled himself through the narrow pointed arch into the tower. Moonlight beamed through a small narrow hole in the roof and thinned the darkness enough so that he could see that no one was within. A wooden ladder against the wall of the tower led to a wooden platform. From this, a guard could observe—and shoot—through any of six ports and cover 360 degrees.

He went out of the tower into the moonlight and signalled. The entire party was soon up on the wall, aided by the ladder which Two Hawks removed from the tower. Gilbert spread his men out so they covered a hundred yards of wall. If the Ikhwani marines tried to scale the walls at this point, the Blodlandish could concentrate a strong fire. Should the Ikhwani try elsewhere along the wall, a sailor in the tower would spot them, provided the Ikhwani were not too far away.

Gilbert, Kwasind, Ilmika, and Two Hawks walked along the passageway until they came to a point beneath which was a gate. Inside the walls was a path that led from the gate on up the mountain. They decided to follow the path. The chances of being ambushed seemed few. It was evident that the Hivika guards had abandoned their posts, the reason for which would have to be determined later.

The path made for easier going even if the slope was as steep as before. By dawn, they were only several hundred yards from the top of the mountain. And here they came across a Hivikan. Sprawled face down by the side of the path, he was dressed in a cloak of brilliant many-colored feathers, a feathered headdress, and a wooden mask set with garnets, turquoise, emeralds. Two Hawks turned the body over and removed the mask. The face of the priest was dark grey. Two Hawks took off his cloak and breastplate of bones and feathers and the cotton skirt. There were no wounds.

Two Hawks' skin prickled, and his head and neck chilled as if a helmet of ice had been placed over them. The others looked as apprehensive as he—all except Kwasind, stolid as ever. Yet he must have been quivering inside, since he was so sensitive to the terrors of the unknown.

Two Hawks started on up but stopped again. The grey light of dawn seemed to be rushing towards certain spots and solidifying. The concentrations, as the party neared them, turned out to be huge statues of grey granite or black basalt or grey porous tufa. They were squat, toadish, and scowling. Most had faces, distorted or misshapen, of men or of gods. Some were of beasts: big-eared, long-snouted, wide-fanged. By the hundreds, they crowded the mountain slope, most of them glaring down the mountain but a few looking upwards.

Kwasind followed Two Hawks so closely he stepped on his heels several times. Two Hawks had to order him back a few paces. "They're only stone," he said. "Dead rocks."

"The rocks are dead," Kwasind muttered. "But what lives within them?"

Two Hawks shrugged and kept on trudging up the steep path at the head of the file. As he ascended, he felt more strongly the broodingness, the almost tangible resentment from the idols. He told himself that it was his own fears working on him; he expected trouble, perhaps death, and the squat grey figures symbolized them. Nevertheless, he was being squeezed around the chest; his breath was coming with more difficulty and his heart was beating harder than the exertions of the climb warranted. He could appreciate and sympathize with the others. Superstitious as they were, they were showing great courage by refusing to bolt.

The rattle of rifle fire broke out far below. It was as if they had been released from a rope that was pulling them the wrong way. All jumped into the air, but their faces showed relief instead of the anxiety that might have been expected. The crack of the battle was such a human, and, to them, mundane phenomenon that it dissipated the strangling psychic air.

Two Hawks looked up and said, "Another hundred yards and we'll be at the cave."

Abruptly, the brown-black, hard-packed dirt of the path ceased. Ahead of him was a dull grey substance that spread out over the mountain from that point up. It felt warm through the sole of his shoe. He told the others to halt.

"Lava," he said. "Still warm."

The stone had flowed down from the mouth of the cave and fanned out to form a triangular apron. The huge entrance to the cave was half-choked with the grey stuff.

"Now we know what scared everybody away," he said. "The Hivika must have thought the mountain was going to blow its top. Or that the gods were angry. Or both. That priest may have died of a heart attack. There's no evidence of poisonous gas."

As they neared the cave, slipping somewhat on the lava, the heat became more intense. Their clothes were soon soaked with sweat, and the bottoms of their feet began to get uncomfortably warm. By the time they reached the entrance of the cave, they knew they could not stay long.

They did not have to linger. The beam of Two Hawks' flashlight into the interior showed the lava sloping sharply upward from the mouth of the cave. Only twenty feet from them, the cave was entirely filled. The eruption—if it was an eruption of Terrestrial origin, had filled the inside. Two Hawks knew from Gilbert's description that the cave extended at least a hundred yards into the stone of the mountain. At the end was—had been—the 'gate.' That is, if it had ever existed.

There was nothing to do now but to forget about the gate and to get away from the Ikhwani. They went back down the path towards the wall. Before they had gotten halfway, they heard the firing cease. Two Hawks stopped them.

"If the Ikhwani have gotten through, they'll be coming up

after us. If they're still being held outside the wall, we can afford to wait a while until we know for sure."

They hid behind a huge stone idol, fifty yards from the path. They leaned against its broad base, ate some dried beef and hard bread, and talked softly. The sun warmed away the chill of night. From time to time, Two Hawks looked around the idol and down the path. He saw nothing for half an hour. Then, he stiffened. Many small figures, shining white and black and scarlet, were toiling up the path. And the sun also twinkled off the barrels of guns or from drawn scimitars.

"Your men have been killed or captured," he said to Gilbert.

Gilbert looked through his binoculars. He swore and then said, "There's a man down there in Ikhwan uniform but wearing Perkunishan medals! His head is bare; he's a blond! From your description, I'd say . . . no, you better look for yourself!"

Two Hawks took the binoculars. When he put them down, he said, "It's Raske."

Ilmika gasped and said, "How could *he* be *here*?"

"Obviously, he got in touch with the Ikhwani embassy in Ireland. He knew where we were going, and he got the Ikhwani to come after me. They want me for the same reason Perkunisha and Blodland did. And if the Ikhwani can't have me alive, they'll have me dead!"

He used the binoculars again and counted thirty-two enemy. There were six men far behind the main body, slow by reason of the two mortars they were carrying. Out on the lagoon, the *Hwaelgold* still rested at anchor and beyond the reef the cruiser prowled back and forth like a restless wolf.

He swept the horizon of the sea. Far out were two plumes of smoke. If only, he prayed, the smoke could be pouring from the stacks of two Hivika warships, hastening to challenge the unauthorized vessels . . . If only . . .

He quit looking. Now was the time to seize all the time they could. He led them back up the mountain until they came to the lava, then turned northward, skirting just below the lava. When they had gotten past it, they began climbing up again, diagonally across the slope.

On rounding the peak, they stopped. The mountain was sheared off here. It fell straight for three thousand feet into the waters of a deep fjord. They would have to climb directly over the top of the peak at the first scalable point—if any.

The Ikhwani had seen them by now and were climbing towards them. They were pushing themselves to the limit and were only three hundred yards below them.

Two Hawks said, "I don't suppose it'd be any worse living in South Africa than elsewhere. But I sure hate to think about learning Arabic; I haven't even mastered Hotinohsonih, Perkunishan, or Blodlandish."

He said to Gilbert, "I'm sure the rest of you will be let go if I surrender to them."

Ilmika said, "What about me, Roger? Would you leave me?"

"Would you come to Ikhwan with me?"

She went into his arms and whispered, "I'll go anywhere you go. Gladly."

"It'd be a miserable lonely life," he said. "The Ikhwan practise a strict purdah, you know."

He released her and swept the sea again with the binoculars. The *Hwaelgold* was aflame; boats were being lowered from it. Water spouts were rising near the merchantman, and smoke puffs from the cruiser. A white sliver with a white wake were departing from the cruiser and headed towards the break in the reef. More Ikhwani marines were on their way. But they'd have to fight through the Blodlandish sailors, who would have established positions by the beach.

The twin smoke feathers on the horizon did not seem to be getting any closer. At this distance and in such a short time, he could not determine how fast or in what direction the unknowns were traveling.

He put down the binoculars and swore. He said, "To hell with the Ikhwani! I'm tired of being passed around like a piece of merchandise! I'm for trying to escape, or, if we're cornered, making a fight of it! The Hivika are bound to come nosing around sooner or later. We can throw ourselves on their mercy!"

Gilbert said, "We'll make them know they're dealing with Blodlandish."

Two Hawks laughed, since there were only two Blodlandish in the group, and one of them was a woman. However, Ilmika was not to be lightly considered. She could outshoot any of the men.

They went back to the point where the mountain became a monolithic verticality. There was a small plateau here about forty yards long and twenty deep. Behind it, was cliff 300 feet high. Below it, the slope was at a 50-degree angle. There were only a few large boulders for cover for the Ikhwani and none whatsoever for a hundred yards just below the plateau. If the marines tried for an approach on the right flank of the defenders, they could get no closer than fifty yards without exposing themselves. And they could get above the defenders only by climbing around the peak. If this were possible, it would still take them many hours.

18

AT ABOUT 1 P.M. the Ikhwani, crawling on their bellies, ventured towards the four large boulders which gave the only protection anywhere near the plateau. By then, the three men had rolled all the boulders on the plateau to its lip. There were ten in all. The defenders placed themselves between some of these and waited. Two Hawks had counted their ammunition and found that there were thirty rounds apiece. He cautioned them against wasting them.

The marines opened the fight with a fusillade that lasted about three minutes. Their bullets keened over the defenders heads, richcheted off the boulders, or struck on the rock below the lip of the plateau. The defenders did not fire back once.

Encouraged by this lack of response, ten marines climbed to the boulders while the rest continued their covering fire. Two Hawks stuck his head out over the lip long enough to see them crawling up. He also observed that the men carrying the mortars had a long way to go. These were very heavy pieces evidently, not like the easily portable field-mortar of his own world.

Two Hawks waited for a few minutes. The firing stopped but he did not look out. When it resumed even more furiously he counted until he thought that the forward line should be at least fifty yards below them. He looked quickly; it was as he had expected. Ten Ikhwani, each separated from the other by ten feet, were advancing. They were on their feet now, crouching, holding their rifles with one hand and getting a grip on rock projections with the other.

He gave a signal. Kwasind and Gilbert got on their knees behind a boulder and shoved it over the lip. It bounded down the mountain like a fox after a hare but struck no one. It did make the marines scatter away from it, however. Two lost their footing and rolled down the slope. By the time they had managed to stop themselves, they were out of the action.

The second boulder knocked an Ikhwan into the air, flipping him over twice before he hit the ground. He did not move thereafter. The marines who had been providing a covering fire were too busy trying to guess which way the boulders would travel. They stopped shooting, and in the interval Two Hawks and Ilmika carefully squeezed off three shots apiece. Four marines were hit. The three survivors started back down the slope. One of them slipped and slid on his face for thirty yards before ramming his head into a small boulder.

"Now they know," Two Hawks said. "If they're smart, they'll wait until the mortars arrive. Then it's good night for us."

Ilmika said, "They don't want you alive, Roger."

"Yes, I know. Raske must have it in for me."

The Ikhwani contented themselves with firing an occasional shot. The mortarmen continued to make progress slowly, even if a number had been sent down to relieve them. Two Hawks estimated that the mortars would not be delivered until close to dusk. Not that night would make much difference in the accuracy of the mortar fire.

He could not see the men from the *Hwaelgold*. The launch from the cruiser had landed long ago and the marines had disappeared into the oak woods. The merchantman had rolled over on its side but was still afloat. And the two pillars of smoke were definitely nearer.

Gilbert told him that the mortars probably had a range of about 200 yards. Two Hawks grinned at this news. To bring the weapons within effective range, the mortarmen would have to leave the protection of the far boulders to station the mortars behind the nearest boulders. He doubted that they would try to do so except under cover of night. They would have too much respect for the stone missiles the defenders could roll down on them.

The sun dropped behind the peak. The blue sky darkened. Two Hawks said, "The moment it gets dark enough, we leave here. The Ikhwani will take some time getting the mortars to those boulders. The others may or may not set up a firing cover for the mortarmen. In either case, we have to take a chance. We'll cut to the right across the slope and hope we can get around the line while they're shooting us up—they'll think."

Clouds from the west came over the mountain, gladdening
the defenders. The sun's influence disappeared entirely, and
a darkness thick as charred jelly covered the mountain. The
four let themselves gingerly over the edge of the plateau and
began crawling down the slope. Approximately a minute later
the night became noisy and flame-shot. The marines were
trying to keep the defenders busy while the mortars were carried to the new positions.

Two Hawks, observing that they were below the line of fire,
changed his mind. He told the others what he wanted to do
but said that they would keep to the original plan if they
preferred. They said they would do what he ordered.

The four began to crawl northeastward, towards the nearest
line of boulders. They arrived there a few minutes before the
mortar crews. On the opposite side of the two boulders, they
listened to the rasp of Arabic while the mortars were being
set up. It was impossible to determine whether only the
mortar crews were there or if others had come with them.
Deciding that the longer he put off action, the less their
chance of surprise, Two Hawks crawled around the huge rock.
He and Ilmika were behind the one; Gilbert and Kwasind
behind the other, ten yards away.

Everything went even better than Two Hawks had hoped.
He shot from one side of the boulder while Ilmika fired from
the other. Kwasind and Gilbert went into action as soon as
they heard the first shot. Although it was dark, the white
trousers and turbans of the marines made for easy shooting.
The four aimed at the dark areas between the white.

There were eight men with each mortar. Four fell at each
mortar before the survivors could bring their revolvers into
play. Several tried to run, slipped, and rolled away out of
the fight. The others died where they stood.

Ilmika and Two Hawks started around the boulder for the
mortar but had to dive for cover. The marines further down,
guessing what had occurred, opened up. Two Hawks' plan of
using the mortars against them, of blasting them off the face
of the mountain with their own weapons, was no longer
feasible. Worse, the marines were advancing towards the
boulders, intent on recapturing the mortars.

The four risked sticking their heads around the boulder
and shooting now and then. But the hail of bullets, screaming
just over their heads, throwing rock chips off the sides of the
boulders, made it suicide to keep on trying a return fire.

Two Hawks cursed. He should have stuck to his original plan. They might be on their way to safety now, if he had not been carried away with his overbold, damned foolish, counterattack.

Suddenly, the racket from below redoubled, tripled in intensity. The bullets stopped flying around them, but the barking bedlam below continued. There were whistles and shouts in a non-Arabic speech. Two Hawks did not understand the words, but he recognized the language as Polynesian.

The Hivika had come.

The battle lasted for about five minutes. Then the surviving Ikhwani surrendered. The Hivika, having been told what was going on by their prisoners, called up for the four to surrender. The officer's Blodlandish was heavily accented, but he could be understood. Gilbert answered in Hivika, and a moment later the four were also prisoners. They joined the others down below.

Raske was there, his hands clasped behind his neck. He laughed when he saw Two Hawks, and he said, "You slippery devil! By the skin of your teeth, heh? You have all the luck of Hitler himself!"

Two Hawks said, "Who's Hitler?"

Postlude

The Norwegian dawn was paling the windows of the hotel room when Two Hawks stopped his narrative.

I said, "Surely you're not going to quit now? Just before the end?"

"I forgot," he said, "that Raske's words would not mean anything to you. At the time he said them, they meant nothing to me. I was too concerned about what was going to become of us to think much about it. All of us, Ikhwani, Blodlandish, Kwasind, Raske, and myself were being tried for illegal entry, a noncapital crime, and for trespassing on sacred ground, a capital crime. But Raske and I had something valuable to offer Hivika in return for our lives. And I got Kwasind and the Blodlandish off, too. However, the king of Hivaka wanted to make an example of somebody, so he hung the Ikhwani marines and also the sailors who had survived the sinking of their ship. Those two smokeplumes I saw came from Hivika cruisers. They sank the Ikhwani ship although not without heavy casualties themselves.

"We spent a year on Hivika, a very busy year, a repetition of what Raske and I had gone through in Perkunisha and Blodland. By the time we got our freedom, the war was over. The plague had finally died out, although not before killing four times as many people in three months as a year of war had done. Perkunisha fell apart; a part of its army and many civilians revolted, a commoner by the name of Wissambr became head of a republic . . . well, you know all this."

"But what's this about . . . a Hitler?" I said.

Two Hawks smiled. "Raske answered that same question for me while we were in the Hivika jail. And he told me about the world from which he had come. As I said, we had always been working too hard while in Berlin to have much small talk or conversation about our lives on what we thought had been the same Earth. Besides, both of us avoided discus-

174

on of our ideologies or goals of our countries. We felt there
as no use carrying on the disputes of a world lost forever
 us.

"It was not until we were in Hivika that we learned that
e had come through the same gate, simultaneously, but
om *different* earths."

"Amazing!"

"Yes. The ruler of the Germany of my world was the
aiser, grandson of the Kaiser of Germany of World War I.
aske said that, in his world, the Kaiser had been exiled to
olland, after World War I. By the way, his World War I
ok place about ten years after that in my world, if your
lative chronologies are correct. In Raske's universe, an
ustrian commoner named Hitler became dictator of Ger-
any and led it into World War II.

"Of course, the World War I of the Kaiser of my world and
 Raske's were not the same people, you understand. They
dn't even have the same personal names. Yet, the course of
story on his world and mine were amazingly similar; the
ople were just different. The coincidences between the two
e too many and too close to be coincidences. So, out the win-
w goes my theory of this earth being populated by humans
ho had passed through gates from my earth.

"Did you know?—no, you wouldn't, of course—that Amer-
an Air Force raids were made on the two Ploestis on the
me day? Raske was in a Messerschmidt, a type unknown
 me, about to attack an American Liberator, much like my
wn bomber, although mine was classed as a Vengeance.

"So—we now know that a 'gate' can open onto more than
vo worlds at once."

There was a knock on the door. He opened it, and the
eautiful Ilmika Thorrsstein entered. She said, "Pardon me,
entlemen, for interrupting, but it is time for us to go."

A moment later, two men came into the room. Two Hawks
troduced me to the herculean Kwasind and the blond and
andsome Raske.

"Where are you going now?" I asked Two Hawks.

"We've heard of something very curious in the glacier
ountry of upper Tyrsland," he said. "The Wakasha nomads
ave stories of strange things in a valley there, of some-
ing that sounds to us like a gate. If the tale has any
undation, you may see us no more. But if it's baseless,
s I expect it will be, then we're staying in this world. Raske

would like to get back to his world, if possible. If he can't he's going to Saariset. He's had a magnificent offer from them; he'll be the next thing to a king if he accepts. Raske, I'm afraid, is the leopard who can't change his spots. As for me, I'll go back to Blodland with Ilmika."

He smiled and said, "This may not be the best of all possible worlds. But it's the one we're in, so we'll make the best of it."

THE END